Raffaella Barker is the author of five acclaimed adult novels, including *Hens Dancing* and *Summertime*. She also writes regularly for *Country Life* and the *Sunday Telegraph*. She was brought up in north Norfolk, not far

Eastern Daily Press

Books for adults by Raffaella Barker

Come and Tell Me Some Lies

The Hook

Hens Dancing

Summertime

Green Grass

RAFFAELLA BARKER

PHOSPHORESCENCE

MACMILLAN CHILDREN'S BOOKS

First published 2004 by Macmillan Children's Books

This edition published 2005 by Macmillan Children's Books
a division of Macmillan Publishers Limited
20 New Wharf Road, London N1 9RR
Basingstoke and Oxford
www.panmacmillan.com

Associated companies throughout the world

ISBN 0 330 41024 5

1 3 5 7 9 8 6 4 2

A CIP catalogue record for this book is available from
the British Library.

Typeset by Intype Libra Ltd
Printed and bound in Great Britain by Mackays of Chatham plc, Kent

For Aurelia and Tallulah with Love

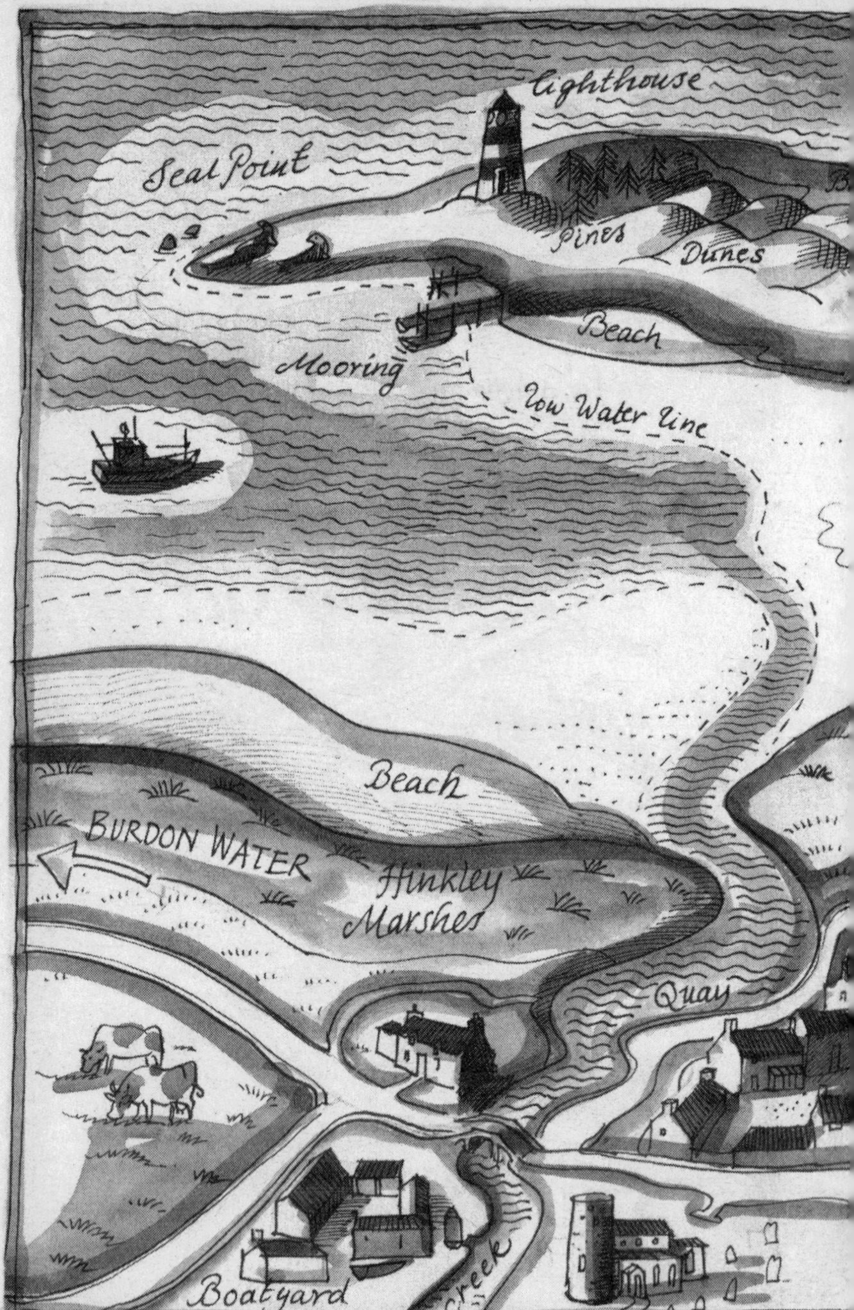
Lighthouse
Seal Point
Pines
Dunes
Beach
Mooring
Low Water Line
Beach
BURDON WATER
Hinkley Marshes
Quay
Boatyard
Creek

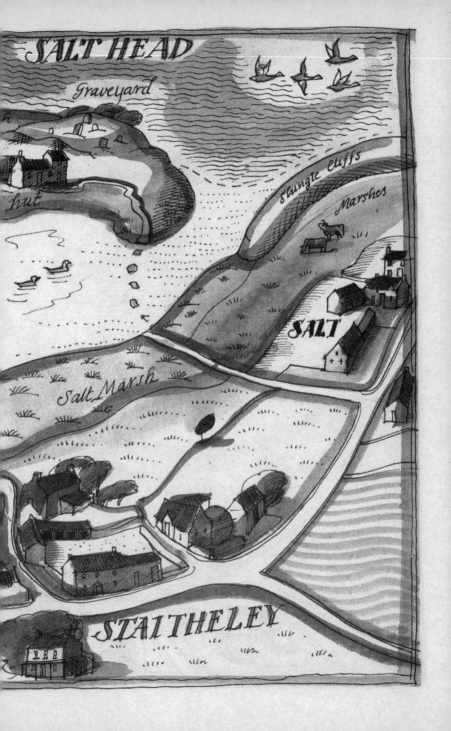

EASTERN DAILY PRESS
15 JULY 1969
FUNERAL
ANNOUNCEMENT

The funeral service for James Jordan, aged 15, who was tragically lost at sea, was held on Friday 12 July at 3.00 p.m. at St Mary's Church, Staitheley.

I t is the first warm day of April, the first possible day of spring, and it is impossible to watch any more telly. I feel as though I have woken from hibernation, and my senses are less slothful than they have been since I suffered the agony of having my ears pierced just before Christmas. Today I can actually smell spring mingling with the salt which is always present in the air here, and the village shop had primroses planted in tubs outside the door. Staitheley is quiet at this time of year, only fishermen are out at sea, and a handful of the heartiest sailors, but everyone else's boats are moored out of the water and lashed with canvas to protect them from the elements. Only the masts clang, a sound as much a part of Staitheley life to me as the call of gulls and the constant rippling whisper of water in the creek.

Staitheley is everyone's favourite place in the summer, when there are holidaymakers and bird-watchers and nature lovers everywhere. The tide floods in and suddenly the sea fills up with boats and the tiny streets are full of people eating ice creams and having barbecues, and laughter echoes off all the cobbled walls as every garden seems to have a party

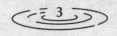

going on in it. When the tide is in, people queue on the quay, waiting for the boats to take them to Salt Head Island and beyond it to Seal Point, to see the famous local seal colony, or as the tide recedes they stay, teetering on the brink of falling in, dangling orange nylon crab lines and scraps of bacon into the muddy water of the harbour. The six weeks of the summer holidays are when most businesses are making their money, but the rest of the time it's dead quiet and I sometimes feel like I am the only living entity, and I have to go into Flixby, our nearest town, to remind myself that there are a few people on the planet beyond the Staitheley pensioners. I usually get Mum to give me a lift to the bus when I want to go and meet my best friend, Nell, there, but today, when I asked Mum, she just yelled, 'You can go on your bike.' Charming. In fact, I'd forgotten I had a bike until she mentioned it and then it took me a while to find it, or rather to get Mum to find it, because it was right back in the back of the garage under a torn sail from my old Laser boat and two rank-smelling lobster pots. Mum always knows where everything is if you keep asking her.

'Look, if you want me to go on my bike, I need to know where it is,' I pointed out, quite reasonably, when I had looked in the obvious places, like outside the back door and outside the front door.

'Why am I the only person who does anything here?' Mum shrieked as she strutted out to the garage. 'It's your father's job to look after bicycles, not mine.'

I think of Dad, out on the Sand Bar at the end of Salt Head, in his waders with his binoculars and

surrounded by screeching birdlife, and I know that he is far too busy taking care of the nature reserve that is the island to ever give any thought to my bike or anyone else's. He didn't even teach me to ride it in the first place – Jack, my grandfather, did that when I was six, and I can remember pedalling along the quay towards Grandma and being full of swooping joy at the new sensation. Dad lives for his job; for him, being warden to the coastline is a vocation, like they say being a nun is. I hope I never get a vocation; I just want a job when I grow up, to get me out and away into the world. Mind you, Mum had a job being a television journalist in London and look where that got her – she met Dad when she came to the North Norfolk coast to make a documentary. They got married and she gave up work when she had me. I think she's a bit frustrated now and it isn't really surprising. She certainly went off on one about my bike today.

'No one is asking you to look after it,' I soothed, 'I just need you to help me find it.'

Mum yanked open the garage door, chucked a few boxes around and located my bike beneath the sail. Unfortunately, seeing the bike didn't improve her temper, and she charged away towards the house again shouting, 'There's the bloody thing and I'm not mending any goddam punctures either.' She should really watch her language. Anyway, I got it out and was delighted that there were no punctures, but no one has been looking after it, least of all me. But now I suppose it isn't surprising that the bike is groaning and listing and its wheel is catching on something,

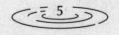

and I've only got a few hundred metres away from home. While I'm glad Mum can't see that I've already ground to a halt, I do also wish she would just drive past in her car and give me a lift to the bus stop after all because I've got to meet Nell, and now I think I'm going to miss the bus.

I gaze up and down the High Street, and as usual there is no one about except a very old lady with a tweed hat on taking a dachshund for a walk. She is Miss Mills from Bridge House, and I hope she can't see this far because I really don't want to talk to her right now. There is a gang of old ladies in Staitheley and they are all friends, or all sworn enemies, of my grandma. She and Jack are not in the thick of it, as they live just out of the village in their house on the edge of the marshes, but she knows every ailment and every complaint that is discussed by the Staitheley ladies. Their three favourite topics are: illnesses, their own and one another's; dogs, and whom they have bitten; and the vicar, Reverend Horace Wells, and what he has done wrong. I have been into almost every old lady's house in Staitheley in the fourteen years of my life, and apart from the holiday-cottage owners who are never here, I know just about everyone in the village. It isn't hard to know everyone because there are a few hundred permanent residents and my dad grew up here too, and my grandfather, so Staitheley is home to my family history as much as it is to me. This is one of the boring things about it.

I would actually like to live in a town where no one has known me since I was a baby, and where cinemas, clothes shops, chemists and cafes lined the

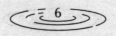

streets. It would be so great if I could go and buy a CD without having to make a special half-day pilgrimage on the bus to Flixby. And it would be great if no one ever made either of the following remarks about me again: 'My, with all that dark hair and those big blue eyes you remind me of your daddy when he was small,' or, 'But look at you now, Lola Jordan, haven't you grown into a fine young lady! I should ask your grandmother to buy you a nice new cardy, you seem to have grown out of that one.' This comment usually comes with a bony old hand prodding my waist which makes me squeal, so the Staitheley grannies think I am a true joker among them and seek me out again and again. It is a big pressure being one of very few children in a very small village. I think it was selfish of Mum and Dad to only have me. A brother or a sister would really take the spotlight off me. Mum is so not sympathetic; whenever I moan, she says I bring it on myself. 'You know you could cover up your midriff when you go round to get Miss Mills's shopping list,' she points out. And she's always telling me to take my coat when taking Enid Selby's naughty West Highland terrier for a walk along with my own darling Jack Russell, and friend through thick and thin, Cactus.

'I could wear old sacks all the time,' I agree, 'but then I wouldn't be being true to myself, Mum.'

That floors her, because Mum's big thing in life is being true to oneself. And communicating. God knows how she manages with Dad because he never communicates anything. He hardly talks. Come to think of it, Mum doesn't talk much to Dad, but she

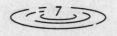

talks to me, and she talks on the phone to her friends in London, especially my Aunt Jane, her sister. Sometimes she cries after that. I think that even after all these years, she misses the excitement of being a working girl in a big city.

Thankfully, Miss Mills has teetered away down towards the quay with Deborah the dachshund undulating along beside her, a bit like a worm on a lead, I always think, but each to her own. Cactus, who is more like a cement-filled rugby ball than a worm, because he is so greedy, is in my rucksack, but I've been hanging around too long and he has noticed a cat. Suddenly he wriggles out and dashes away after it. He vanishes down one of the little alleyways that criss-cross between walled gardens and courtyards which make up the heart of Staitheley and that I am sure must have been built by smugglers no matter how Dad insists they were just for taking coal to houses. Anyway, I can't be bothered to go after Cactus. He'll just go home when he's finished hell-raising and I'll see him when I get back. No one can get lost in our village, so I never worry about him.

Staitheley is small. It still spans both sides of the creek but once, as Dad has told me more times than I can be bothered to remember, it was a great port. All that is left of the port now is the quay and the merchants' houses that line it. They face out across the salt marshes to the limitless sea, as if protecting the flint cottages clustered between the two main streets, which reach back from the quay like arms wrapped around the heart of Staitheley.

'There is nothing between us and the North Pole,'

Dad likes to tell me. In the winter I have no trouble believing him. Dad knows everything about this coastline and its web of creeks, which flow through the salt marshes, flooding them with the incoming tide and receding again when the tide ebbs so that mousse-thick mud oozes wherever you walk. It always feels to me like the marshes and the island, Salt Head, belong to Dad and not to the Trust for whom he works. Occasionally he puts on a tie with his tweed jacket and goes to their head office in Cambridge for a meeting, where they ask him stuff like, 'Where is the erosion happening?' or, 'Do you have a policy on pollution?' but mainly they just leave him to manage it for them and so the huge sweep of sometimes land (low tide) and sometimes sea (high tide) which stretches from the tiny village of Salt along the coast to the west part of Staitheley and on to Hinkley Marshes and Beetley Creek and the weirdly popular village of Burdon Water is Dad's kingdom.

When I was much younger, as soon as I could come back from school I would run up to Dad's study, where the curved window and the large telescope gave a wide panoramic view of the marshes. If I saw his familiar figure somewhere out on the edge of the water, light dancing silver streaks around him, I would hurry out with Cactus, following the path between pink-tinged heather clumps, sometimes taking half an hour or more to reach him.

These days I find some parts of Dad's job really embarrassing: for example, in the summer he drives around with binoculars on the beaches and if he sees

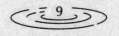

a plume of smoke he zooms across and throws sand over people's barbecues.

'I'm sorry, it's the Trust's policy, and we've had problems with fire every summer,' he always says. If they're understanding and easy with him, he stands at a distance and lets them finish cooking, but if they're rude or try to threaten him, he pours a bottle of water right into the flames and he doesn't even move the sausages or whatever they're cooking. I try to avoid going with him when he's doing this sort of beach patrol, it's just too cringe-making, and I don't like to get involved when he takes school parties out on to Salt Head and he tells his repertoire of a whole lot of lame jokes which I have heard too many times before. But when we go out on our own together, and he shows me where the seals go to have their pups and he tells me how a sea mist comes in on a hot summer day when the wind is in the north, I am caught up in the magic of the coast that is my home and I succumb to its spell. Today is not magical, although spring beckons. A cloud like a purple bruise hangs over the village. The air is mild and the wind has dropped to a breeze which catches my hair and whips it into my eyes.

I wiggle the front wheel of my bike hopefully. Perhaps it will fix itself in a minute. A boy skims past on a skateboard, but U-turns gracefully back to me.

'What's happened?' He crouches by my bike. He has thick hair flopping over his forehead and I am struck too by the hollow of his cheekbone and his mouth. He looks at me and a grin bursts on my face involuntarily and unstoppably. I can't stop grinning as he takes my bike and turns it upside down on the edge of the road. In fact I have to turn away and push my hair back from my face, dragging my hands across my eyes and mouth to make myself sensible again. A small self-administered slap helps, but I have a sneaking feeling that he might have seen me do it. So now he will think I am a total weirdo. I turn back to him, suddenly aware again that he is very kindly fixing my bike and needs praise and attention.

'You've bent the wheel,' he says, spinning it with his hand flat, hovering just above the ridged rubber of the tyre. 'Come back with me, and I can fix it for you in the workshop.' He gestures over his shoulder. I know where he is pointing. I know who he is. How could I not in such a small village? His name is Josh Christie, and his dad is a fisherman and a boatbuilder called Ian. The Christies used to live a few miles away in a smaller village than Staitheley but recently they moved into a big boatyard which sprawls on to the road between wide cobbled walls just along the quay from our house. I know all about them, or a version of them, because Ian Christie grew up with my dad, and they were friends once.

Josh gives me his skateboard to carry, and he wheels my bike into the boatyard. In the open shed, the hull of a boat is suspended from ropes that are wrapped around the beams, and curls of wood shavings litter the floor. Outside, a line of different-coloured buoys glow red and orange against the flint wall. I have been to this boatyard many times, before the Christies came to live here, but now my dad prefers to drive to Salt. He avoids Ian Christie like a

11

bad smell, and says I'm imagining it when I challenge him. I can't be bothered with the way grown-ups fall out. It obviously happens more and more as you get older; just look at all my grandma's cronies, arguing and having feuds. Everyone knows everyone here, and although I find it pretty annoying at times, mostly it is a friendly feeling.

Josh has the wheel off my bike, and whistling absently he clamps it into a vice on the workbench.

'How do you know what to do?'

I wasn't really expecting to bump into a boy today, especially not Josh Christie, although as he is the only boy anywhere near my age around the village, I suppose he is the only one I am at all likely to see. But me and Nell, who is the person apart from Cactus that I am closest to on earth, and who I have sat next to at school in every class since we started at primary together, have been eyeing him up on the bus for a while. Not that he'd have noticed us lowly fourteen-year-olds. But it's so weird that now here he is, very interested in my bike but not actually saying anything to me. The silence yawns between us and I babble to fill it.

'I'm catching the bus to Flixby to meet my friend Nell at the cinema. Do you want to come?'

Ohmigod. I have to dig my fingernails into the palm of my hand to stop myself apologizing straight away, and I bite my lip so as not to take the words back. That will only make things worse. Of course he will say no. What an idiot I am. Nell will crucify me. I can just imagine exactly what she'll say: 'You can't just invite boys to come to the cinema with you! It's

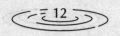

like going on a date, to be anywhere near a cinema with a boy. You know that, Lola, don't you?'

Josh straightens up from gazing intently at the vice and the bent wheel and looks at me.

'What are you going to see?'

'Err, umm, yess . . .' Oh God. Why did I say the cinema? I suppose it made sense because it is where I'm meeting Nell, but we haven't planned to actually *see* anything. We might go to Woolworths and look through the CDs. Maybe buy one. But seeing a film? Not a priority today, not with only five pounds left to last me until the end of the holidays, unless I get a job. I could kick myself. Of course he would want to know what we are seeing. What might be on? Think of a film. There must be a film title somewhere in my brain. Any old one will do. I shift from foot to foot, rolling my eyes. Josh, looking perplexed, stares at me then turns back to the wheel.

'I've straightened this, and I've moved the brake pads, so I think it'll be OK now.'

He begins to untwist the vice, spinning the bar, bouncing the tyre and whistling.

'Oh no!' Accidentally my thoughts erupt out of my mouth: the only film title to ping into my otherwise blank and panicking mind is a French one. The one I read the review of this morning in the paper. How could anyone possibly try to speak even two or three French words to a boy they have just met? I'll have to get round it somehow.

'It's that French one about . . . about . . .' Shit! I should never have pursued this line of chatting. Never. The French film is about kissing. Nothing else,

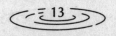

just kissing. The reviewer was scathing about it. Said it was a teen flick all dressed up and nowhere to go and it would give you glandular fever just to watch it. Oops, how do I convey this to Josh without mentioning anything about snogging? Impossible. Gulping, I grab the handlebars of the bike as Josh tightens the last nut, and mumble, 'Better go. Thanks. G'dbye.'

'Hey. Wait.' Josh stands in front of my bike, blocking the path to the road. His hair flops across his forehead, and he pushes it back impatiently. 'I'd like to see the French film. I'll meet you outside the cinema at two o'clock.' He grins suddenly. 'You do mean the one about . . . ?' and he pauses, his eyes lit with laughter.

I can feel my face turning scarlet. I press my hands on my cheeks, but I feel as if I am about to melt, and escape is the only answer. Anyway, I am late for the bus. I'm going to have to pedal like a lunatic to get there on time. I swing up on to the bicycle and, wobbling into my stride, say, as casually as I can muster, 'Mmm. Yes. That one. I'm really glad you can come. Good.'

So off I go, blathering away like a total idiot, as I explain to Nell in Burger King opposite the cinema. Nell drains her Coke and rolls the paper beaker along the table towards me. 'Well, you're not a total one hundred per cent idiot, because he's coming, isn't he?'

Mindlessly, I roll the cup back. 'I don't suppose he'll turn up.'

'Well, so what?' Nell stands up, looking at her

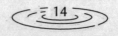

watch. 'It's not like we came specially to meet him, or planned the whole thing around him, is it? If he doesn't come, we're saved the embarrassment of sitting with a boy watching snogging for two hours.'

Collapsing on one another, giggling, we stagger out and across the road to the cinema. No one is waiting for us by the door.

'He's late,' I point out. Nell does not reply. I nudge her. 'He's late, I said. I don't think he's coming. We should go in or we'll miss it.'

Nell grabs my hand and pinches it.

'No he's not late,' she says under her breath. 'He's there.'

The Hollywood cinema fills the block in the small terraced side street of Flixby. At one end the road gives way to the main street down to the station, at the other a car park defined by high flint walls is the site of the Tuesday market. Today, though, under the spilling weight of a blossom-heavy cherry tree, a small, dark blue motorbike has drawn up. Opening the box on the back of the bike, the rider takes off his helmet and gloves and stows them away before turning towards the cinema, unzipping his jacket as he approaches. It is Josh.

How could anyone have ever imagined that Josh Christie would become friends with me? Nell says it's because it's the holidays and none of his friends live as near as I do, but she admitted she was only jealous, so I just giggle when she says it on the phone a week after the cinema. As I put the phone down and rush

through the kitchen, I shout to Mum, 'I'm going round to the Christies for tea.'

Mum is lying on the sofa doing nothing, which seems to be the way she spends most of her time at the moment. In a way I am grateful because it means she isn't being nosy about my life. Normally she would want to know what it was like there, what we talk about and, nosiest of all, what I feel about Josh. Mum is one of those people who like to talk about feelings. She used to hate me watching television on Saturday mornings until one day she sat with me through an episode of *Sabrina, the Teenage Witch*, where Sabrina went on a Guilt Trip on a bus. Mum was fantastic.

'God, I wish there'd been programmes like that in my day to help me deal with adolescence,' she said after the programme was finished. 'Tell me, Lola, how do you sort out that sort of thing? Are you and your friends open about it?'

'Er, yup.'

I am hoping this is the answer which will get her off my back quickest. Sometimes I feel she is trying to get a torch and look at all the corners of my mind that I don't think about, and I wish I was not an only child so there'd be someone else for her to focus her attention on. Or else I wish she would get a job, but when I suggest it, she rolls her eyes and says, 'There isn't much I can do here apart from waitressing in the pub. The media world is limited to the church newsletter and I don't think Enid Selby would like me to help with that, do you?'

It's true, I can't see Mum reporting on local jam

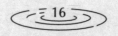

sales at the Women's Institute and taking what she finds out back to Mrs Selby, widow of a former rector, to edit for her. It is a long way from news documentaries, I guess. She may as well stick with the self-help books I have noticed piling up around her bed. The latest is called *Boundaries: Where I End and You Begin*. I am grateful to this book, however daft it sounds, because I think it must be what has stopped her cross-questioning me about Josh.

It is only a few minutes from my house on the quay to the Christies' and I run most of the way, wanting as much time there as possible today because tomorrow I am meant to start work on Salt Head with Dad. He's going to pay me to help him log the birds and other wildlife for one week. He is supposed to be doing some sort of report for English Nature about the seals and their environment. Although I love it on the island, and I have been looking forward to working with Dad, I am a bit torn now. I just want to hang out with Josh and Nell and listen to music and stuff. I have spent so much of my time with Dad out on the marshes, I can't help feeling it will be a bit lonely and quiet. And I'll have to wear wellies and an anorak all the time, which is such a waste of all the new clothes I bought with my Christmas money and have hardly worn as I am always in school uniform or wet-weather kit.

Josh's mum, Caroline, is making bread when I arrive there, and the kitchen is warm and friendly and very untidy.

'Hello, Lola, come and have some tea.' She

smiles, and I sit down in front of a patch of flour. 'Do you fancy doing some kneading?'

She gives me a piece of dough, and I cut a bit off for Sadie, Josh's five-year-old sister, who has sidled up next to me.

'What shall we make?' Sadie whispers. She has the cutest dimples. I grin at her and we start making a fat dough mermaid. Something about Caroline is so warm and encouraging that I start telling her about the work I am meant to be doing.

'I feel a bit guilty saying to Dad that I don't want to do it, and it would be nice to have the money,' I explain, almost telling myself as much as her, 'but he only gave me the job to be kind, because he doesn't really need me. There is a proper student coming to help tomorrow. He just thinks he shouldn't let me down.'

Caroline squidges the dough into bread tins and slides them into the oven. She looks at me with a kind of arrested expression then she says, 'Lola, I've got an idea. Why don't you work for me? I need some help with Sadie this holidays while we are getting the sailing school up and running. I can help Ian in the office if you could have Sadie for a few hours every day.'

I cannot believe my luck. To be paid for looking after Sadie, who is really adorable, in Josh's house with Josh around is brilliant.

Nell is almost sick with envy when I phone her to tell her.

'You are so lucky living up there; I wish I could

18

get a holiday job like yours, I have to do a lame paper round in Flixby.'

'Well, come and help me. Sadie will love there being two of us,' I suggest.

And often there is Josh. He seems to be here all the time and Sadie skips up to him when he is standing eating cereal by the Aga or taking the wheels off his skateboard to clean some tiny cog, and she tells him jokes and climbs his legs, with her hands in his, to do a somersault. I feel sad that I have no brother when I see them together, and I almost can't stop thinking about him when I am not there. But he is seventeen and I can tell that he thinks of me more as an extension of Sadie than a fit female. On my third day of looking after Sadie, she comes to greet me at the door dressed for a deluge.

'I've got my wet-weather clothes on because Josh is taking us to Seal Point and we're having elevenses,' she announces. I grin madly and whirl her into my arms to hug her. This is perfect, just me and Josh and Sadie. Almost before the excitement can engulf me my heart starts pounding. Only me and Josh and Sadie for a whole morning. How will we keep talking? I won't be able to think of anything to say and we will have to shout anyway above the engine and it will take hours to get there.

Josh is on the quay in the boat. It is a very ordinary, grey workboat with 'Staitheley Sailing School' painted down its side. Josh is checking the fuel tank attached to the large outboard engine. His hands are brown and he has a faded green-and-silver woven plait of thread around his wrist. My stomach somersaults and I wish I could control myself and not feel like a tongue-tied idiot.

'I love the seals and the seals love me.' Sadie skips on to the boat and sits down in the bow, pulling three Barbies out of her pocket and arranging them so that they are perched with their heads looking over the side.

'Can you untie us?' Josh starts the engine while I untwist the rope from the cleat on the dockside and we chug out of the harbour, cutting through the smooth grey water, making slow headway towards Salt Head Island and the seals beyond.

Salt Head is not always an island as you can wade out to the eastern end at low tide. There's a path across the marshes from Salt, with warning notices about the dangers of being caught by fast incoming tides. At the opposite end of Salt Head is the Sand Bar, with its colony of seals.

The seals are a real attraction for tourists, and in Staitheley there are two different businesses running trips out to see them. We are friends with them both, but closest to the Lawsons, two brothers in their twenties who used to babysit me when I was small. I usually get a ride with them if I want to go out round the end of Salt Head. Today their boat is way ahead of ours, and its red bulk is a bright but distant beacon in the heavy flat sea.

Seal Point is a sandbank beyond the island and it isn't really anywhere most of the time because it is underwater, but at low tide it is exposed and the seals from the Sand Bar go and loll there on the warm wet sands. I don't go out there on my own because it is too far for my small Laser and the currents are dangerous. Dad won't let me, so it feels very liberating to be heading off there with just Josh in charge.

Josh still hasn't looked directly at me and we have been in the boat for ages – at least twenty minutes I should think. Sadie is singing to her Barbies, and I gaze out at the horizon with a totally blank mind.

Josh leans towards me and shouts, 'Have you heard about the whale?'

'What whale? Is it a joke?' I shout back, and suddenly the ice between us is broken and we both laugh and begin to talk, and once we start we are so easy with one another I feel I have been chatting to him like this all my life. He tells me that a thirty-foot dead whale has been beached further up the coast and people have got caught by the tide wading out to see it. We reach the seals at lunchtime and the water is so clear that we can see their black torpedo bodies as they zoom beneath our boat to emerge, popping up in the sea, with amiable sleek faces which Sadie is convinced are smiling at her.

'Look – that one is Starburst. I named him last time when Josh and Daddy brought me. He wants to play with Barbie.' And without so much as a last goodbye, she flings one of her three Barbies into the water.

Josh and I look at one another and the moment is intense before we burst out laughing.

'Do you live with the Christies now?' Dad asks

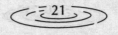

sharply at supper one evening a week later. 'You haven't been here for days.'

I spear a cherry tomato and eat it before answering.

'They're really busy getting the boats ready. The sailing school's starting any time now and Caroline – I mean Mrs Christie – is doing all the admin for it. It's going to be brilliant.'

Dad puts down his knife and fork with a clatter.

'It makes life awkward. I would have thought Caroline would realize that,' he mutters. I stare at him.

'Why is it awkward? I'm good with children. I love Sadie and it's really nice at their house – no one is in a bad mood all the time.'

I am so sick of Dad looking gloomy. I think he might be ill. He used to come home with things he had found to show me and with stories about everyone in the village and lists of things that needed doing. He was the person the old ladies would ask about fixing a gate or putting up a noticeboard, but now he is morose and silent and he doesn't call Miss Mills back when Mum tells him she telephoned to ask him about the date of the next Parish Council Meeting.

Mum looks at him across the table and her eyes are hard.

'Come on, Richard, lighten up,' she says.

Dad pushes his plate away and gets up. He puts on his coat and goes out, calling Cactus to follow him into the dark. Sighing, Mum takes both her plate and his to the sink and I am left, looking at the last two

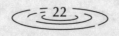

tomatoes in the bowl in front of me, alone at the kitchen table.

'I've got to go too,' I mutter, 'I'm babysitting,' and I rush out of the door.

At the moment I really don't like being at home. It is so silent: Mum is always sighing or just lying on the sofa with no lights turned on, and Dad is always out.

Tonight when I arrive at Josh's house to bath Sadie and put her to bed, the noisy chaos of the Christie kitchen envelops me like a warm embrace. The telephone is ringing, Neoprene the African grey parrot is singing a nursery rhyme Sadie has taught him, and Josh is practising guitar chords, settled deep in the sagging sofa beneath the kitchen window. Caroline answers the telephone as I arrive, but she finishes her conversation and comes back to the table, pushing wisps of wild hair back from her face, which is pink and friendly as she smiles a welcome to me and carries on her conversation with Ian. He is smoking a cigarette, his chair back from the table, and he has managed to get himself looking very relaxed in what must be an uncomfortable position for a tall man, on a small kitchen chair, stretched out with his ankles crossed miles in front of him. They are talking about the advertising brochure for the sailing school.

'I think we should have a picture of Josh and you on the front,' Caroline says, teasing her husband, 'wearing stripy T-shirts or smocks and looking nice and nautical.'

'No way,' Josh interrupts. 'Put Dad in the picture

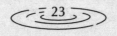

with Neoprene. Sailors should have parrots, shouldn't they?'

Ian laughs and suggests, 'Maybe you, Caroline, wearing your bikini, might attract more clients?'

Even though Caroline is not the bikini type, she doesn't seem to be offended in the general laughter and the phone rings again. Sadie picks it up.

'Hello. This is Sadie's house. I'm five and they're all Loony Toons here. Who is that anyway?' she warbles before anyone else can grab the receiver.

2

My family life is small and contained, just Mum and Dad and me. Dad is away so much at the moment, or about to go. I keep on tripping over his bag, and Cactus looks upset whenever he sees it out again.

'Well, you're never here, so how does it affect you?' I ask Dad, after he moans that I have spent three evenings out of four with the Christies this week. 'The only person at home any more is Mum.'

Dad is taken aback. 'Well, the Trust has huge planning meetings at this time of year.' He shifts in his chair by the fire, dropping his newspaper on to his chest, stretching out his feet. I have to look away when I notice he is wearing his horrible, old-man slippers. 'There's a lot to plan for this year, but as soon as the days are longer I'll be back on the marshes.' He smiles an end-of-conversation smile and turns back to his paper. The door to the kitchen clicks shut, and from behind it come muffled sounds: the flump of the fridge door and the clatter of a pan as Mum begins to clear away supper, the click of her heels on the stone floor. I open the door to join her, and I catch her, red-eyed, crying. Her quiet, secret crying makes me uneasy.

'What's the matter, Mum? Why are you unhappy?'

She shakes her head and manages a sad, small smile.

'I'm not, love, I'm fine,' she insists. 'I've just got backache.'

Frankly, I'm not surprised. She must do her back in completely. Even though everyone else in Staithe-ley wears sensible shoes, Mum is never out of proper heels unless there is an actual flood to prevent her. She still wears urban shoes and clothes, even after all these years on the edge of the sea. I've never seen her in slippers and her wellies are fifteen years old but they still look brand new.

'It's probably your shoes,' I suggest, wiping dishes and placing them back in the cupboard.

'Yes, I expect it is,' she agrees quietly, 'I'm sure you are right.'

Mum is sad and quiet now, but she used to be happy, I think. She says she has no one to talk to but fish, and it's true that if you draw a circle, with our house as the mid-point, more than half the circle would be in the sea. When I was small I played on the quay every day, fishing for crabs, and I didn't know any other children in the village, so I did everything with Mum, and that's when I can remember her really laughing and happy. But I remember that even when I was small, I was always waiting for the day when I could go off across the marshes with Dad, and Jack, my grandfather, and Mum never wanted to do that.

She really wanted a life in a town with a garden and a road outside leading to friends and shops, not a small seaside house with markers to show the height the floods might reach, and a creek full of mud and salt water outside the back door. Mum feels hemmed in by the sea, and Dad feels free. That's how different they are. I think I am somewhere in the middle, which makes sense, I suppose.

Mum says the sea is a fair-weather friend and a cruel enemy, and she is right. Every day the turning tide is a reminder of Dad's older brother James, drowned when he was fifteen and the boat he was sailing with his best friend, Ian Christie, was swept out and around Seal Point on a rip tide, and further into a storm where it capsized, tossing James far out into the cold, roaring sea. Ian was picked up by the lifeboat, but it was a week before James's body was found, carried miles down the coast by the powerful currents. Not having any brothers or sisters, I can't properly imagine what it would be like to lose one, but when I am with Grandma and I find her looking at the photograph of James smiling, holding up a huge sea trout he caught on his fourteenth birthday, sadness runs through my veins like ice.

I know because Mum told me that the reason why Dad doesn't talk to Ian Christie is that he has never been able to get over his brother's death. Dad was only twelve, and tagged along with James and Ian wherever they went. He could so easily have been with them that day, but he was at home with Grandma. I don't think he can forgive himself for that either, or that's what Mum says. It's funny,

because Mum talks to me about this, and tells me what she thinks Dad and Grandma feel about it, and what she thinks Jack might feel, but none of them ever say anything about it themselves. It is a secret that everyone knows.

The next afternoon I walk across the marshes to my grandparents' house. Ever since I was little I have spent a night there every week, but these holidays I've been too busy and my old familiar routine has disappeared. I have been feeling a bit guilty about not seeing them, but Grandma hugs me and smiles and I know I don't ever have to apologize because she is glad to see me.

Jack, my grandfather, white-haired, gruff, but kind, and with a big moustache, has always lived on the marshes, and now he is nearly eighty. He has been a fisherman all his life and he is still out setting mussel and lobster traps on every tide. He has caught every kind of fish there is to find in these waters and he is famous in all the villages around here for bringing in a catch on tides when most people wouldn't dare leave the harbour.

'He's an old fool,' snaps Annie, my grandma. 'He has no need to be out there in all weathers now. He could come and help me in the garden, but he's always got a boat to mend or an engine to restore.'

I love Grandma's house, where the kitchen is warm with the scent of clean laundry and baking, and there are tins in the cupboard by the window always full of the flapjacks and cakes she makes. In the telly room, which Grandma calls the drawing room, a high shelf around the walls gleams with

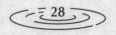

pearl-pink lustre china, and there is a box of toys kept behind the sofa for visiting children; in other words, mostly for me. The toys in it are battered and faded survivors from Dad's childhood, growing up here on the marshes with his two older brothers, John and poor lost James. It makes me sad to see them gathering dust, unplayed with in the box, so I always get them out when I am at Grandma's.

I have developed a ritual with the toys. I separate them into the groups I think suit the three brothers or what I know of them. In Dad's lot, for example, I put all the animals: the lead donkey with the carrot in its mouth, the cattle and the sea lion with its bucket of fish. Of course, there aren't many wild sea birds in a children's farmyard collection, but there are a few trees and the odd tiny painting, on scraps of crumpled paper, of a garden or a field. I add all these things, and I like to think you could get a sense of Dad and his connection with nature, when you look at the toys I give him. In James's pile I sort all the little boats and their fishing nets, the miniature lighthouse and the tiny toy ice-cream van. Anything with a connection to the sea, because all I know about him is that he loved being on the water, and even that is more something I know in my head, because no one ever talks about him to me. I feel sad when I think of James, so any random black toys tend to go in his pile, like the plastic alien that appeared in the box one day, and the model Batman figure. Dad got the Bart Simpson model that came out of a cereal packet, and I gave John the McDonald's plastic car. When James died, John, the oldest of the three, was nineteen, and the tragedy made him closed and silent. He would not go on the sea again, no matter how Jack shouted and blustered and tried to persuade him to help with the boats. John moved away when he left school, to landlocked Germany, and began working in electronics. So his toys must be the cars and tractors, the engines and wheels and dynamos in the wooden box. I line them all up, and then, because I don't know what else to do, and I am not interested in them at all, I make myself play with them and I vroom them around the room until Grandma finds me for tea and says, 'Aren't you a bit old for those toys now?' But I like them because they give me a secret entrance into the past.

My Uncle John rarely comes back to Staitheley. Sometimes he sends me gadgets, and I struggle to see what they are for. But if I ask Dad, he gazes at them, baffled, and smiles wryly before saying, 'I think we'll take this to Jack. He knows how things work.'

Every time I go over to Salt Head with Jack he shows me something I haven't seen before or tells me something new. You would think he would run out of things, but an island is always changing, and he has such a knack for finding curious things washed up by the tide that I used to sometimes think he'd come along for a rehearsal before bringing me.

Once we found a wooden chessboard under a twist of rope at the very end of the northernmost beach; another time after terrible electric storms and high seas for weeks, we found a wedding dress, or the ragged remains of one. I shiver slightly with this memory. It is so vivid it could have been yesterday, but it was four years ago. It was a summer afternoon, and Jack and I had taken Cactus for a walk at the northern tip of the island. The tide was coming in, and we had taken my little red boat with its outboard motor.

'Let's go up and see what the storms have done round the end of the island. We'll wave to your father. I know he went over there this afternoon.'

We chugged up the inside channel past the marshes, with Jack showing me nests abandoned by the oystercatchers because of the unusually high water. Leaning out with the binoculars, I was exclaiming over a nest, 'Oh, it's got eggs in. She must be going back. Look, Jack.'

I turned round when he didn't answer, and his face was blank white and he was staring at something in the water.

'What is it? Tell me? Let me see.'

Jack tried to stand between me and the edge of the boat.

'NO, sit down and keep yourself quiet,' he said sharply, but it was too late.

Floating lazily on a wave, not more than four metres away, was a soft, mist-white shape, spreading and undulating on the water. My heart hammered in my throat. I slipped my hand into Jack's and stepped closer to him.

'It's fabric.' His voice was gruff, but I could hear relief in it. 'Just fabric. You know how storms throw things up.' Whatever Jack had feared had now passed. He was back in control. Reassured by the timbre of his voice, I leaned over the edge, craning to see.

'It's lacy, it looks like a tablecloth or something, it's all lacy. Pass me a pole, Jack, let's hook it in, it might be a treasure.'

'I think not.' Jack's hand was under my arm now, steering me back from the mass in the water.

He was still pale, and he folded his mouth firmly shut as he opened the throttle and we left the inexplicable lace floating on the sea. No one would speculate with me as to what it might be, everyone was playing down its interest and importance back home, and I soon forgot about it. But later that week, Dad's friend Billy Lawson came round with some shrimps and told Dad he'd found a wedding dress.

'It was hooked up in my pots. Gave me one helluva shock, I'll tell you. People say it was from up the coast. Some honeymoon yacht in trouble, everyone drowned.'

Dad and Billy were on the doorstep talking, and I was in my room with the window open. But I leaned out to listen, and shouted down in excitement and dread, 'That's what me and Jack saw, we saw the wedding dress. Is the bride dead?'

Dad and Billy looked up, startled to see me. Dad rammed his cap on his head, a sign he was ready to leave. 'No, she's not. People love to make up stories. I doubt it is actually a wedding dress, it's probably some old rubbish that has been dumped. I shall ring the Port Authorities to find out what ships have been in the area making a mess.' And with an expression of finality Dad marched off with Billy in tow.

Jack though was definitely still shocked. I saw it when I went to tell him what Billy had said, and he

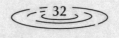

suddenly looked frail. 'Don't go listening to gossip,' he said mildly. 'You come and help me with these nets and take your mind off that sort of nonsense.'

Thinking back now, I realize that was the first time I saw any sign of Jack being old. I don't notice it any more, but then I haven't seen Jack and Grandma much because I have been working. Suddenly my life does not revolve around my family; I am part of the Christies' world this holidays.

Caroline Christie gives me lots of work so I am saving up quite a bit of money. I thought being around Josh all the time was going to turn our friendship into a swoony romance like a photo love story, but actually he has become more like I reckon a brother would be. Nell is here quite a lot too, and the three of us go out on our bikes, with Sadie on Josh's crossbar. Today we go up to Salt and have hot chocolate in the bird-watchers' cafe.

'Sadie, you mustn't tell Mum,' Josh warns her, adding some marshmallows to her fistful of sugar lumps in a blatant attempt to buy her silence.

'Tell Mum what?' Sadie flings the marshmallows into her cup and stirs it vigorously, spilling a lot of the steaming contents. 'I haven't got anything to tell her, have I?' She blinks innocently at her brother.

Nell is gazing at her adoringly, but I whisper, 'Don't be misled. She's very crafty. Watch her black-mail him now.'

'No,' Josh agrees, 'but Mum will go into a total psych if she finds out we brought you along the road

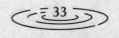

on my bike, so you can't say you came here for hot chocolate, OK?'

'I could forget, you mean?' Sadie is thoroughly enjoying the attention.

'Honestly,' Nell whispers. 'She sounds like someone in a gangster movie.'

'Yes.' Josh struggles to retain control of the situation. 'Just forget we came here.'

'I could,' Sadie muses. 'But I might need some cake to remind me to forget.' And watching our faces as we try not to laugh, she bangs her small fist on the table and cackles, loving her power. 'I see you smiling, Josh, and you, Lola! Ha ha.'

'The only way to survive extortion is to own up,' I say. 'I'll tell Caroline it was me.'

'OK,' Josh agrees, 'that's fine. My mum loves you.'

'What's extortion?' asks Sadie.

Sure enough, Caroline laughs when I tell her what Sadie said.

'Oh, she's so lucky to be having all this fun with you, Lola. I don't know what I would do without you. We'll have to see if you can't carry on coming a bit in term time, or we'll all miss you.'

The next day is a day I can remember every moment of. Sadie and I come in from crab fishing, and for once I bring her to our house because she's really wet and cold and it's right next to the quay. In fact, I brought her home because I thought Mum would like to meet her. Sadie is sitting at the kitchen table, twizzling her plaits while I make her some toast, when Mum comes in. Sadie is in full flow of a story about her crab, who is in a bucket on the table in front of her.

'He's waving at me. Look at his claws, they're toes really, aren't they? I love that crab, Lola. His name is Jeffrey Johnson.' She squeals, blowing him kisses from a safe distance. 'He's my pet. I'm going to keep him in the cage with Neoprene. They can be best friends.'

The toast pops up and I butter it, not noticing Mum come into the kitchen because I am listening to Sadie.

Mum is suddenly right behind me. 'Lola. I have to talk to you. I'm so sorry, darling. I don't know how you will react to what I am going to say, but please try to remember that I love you.'

I am instantly afraid, and I don't know what I am afraid of but it is making my heart bang against my chest so hard I am amazed Sadie can't hear it.

Startled, I turn to face her.

'I'd better take Sadie home,' I mutter, and picking up Sadie and the bucket containing Jeffrey Johnson, I shoot out of the house. I don't know what Mum's going to say, but I don't think Sadie needs to hear it.

'Your mum's got sad eyes,' Sadie observes into my ear as I scuttle along the pavement with her held tight in my arms, the water from the crab bucket slopping over my feet. 'She can't help crying, can she?'

Tears of sympathy for poor Mum well up, and I just post Sadie through the front door with Jeffrey Johnson and shout, 'Here she is, sorry, must go!' before slamming out again. Miss Mills waves to me just as I am reaching our gate, and I wave back,

smiling my biggest smile, even though she is half blind, and I very much doubt she can see my face properly. I want so badly to believe that everything is all right.

Mum has made a pot of tea and cleared away Sadie's toast. I look at the shiny dark surface of the kitchen table where everything is tidy, and tears begin to drip down my face because I know nothing is going to be the same any more, and I can suddenly feel the huge weight of my mum's unhappiness.

She takes my hand in both of hers.

'Dad and I have both decided that we can no longer remain married,' she says.

Is that how most people do it, then? Is there a set line that they look up in some sort of handbook for parents who want to break up? I know the next line, and yes, here it comes.

'But we both love you, and none of this is to do with you, it's to do with us.'

Huh! How can it possibly not be to do with me when I am one of 'us'? 'Us' is my dad, my mum and me, it always has been. It always was.

On Mum goes, and to be honest, I can hardly hear what she is saying because my head is whirling. She squeezes my hand and tries to look jaunty by tousling her pale hair with her other hand. She flashes her eyes at me, and, frankly, looks mad as she announces, 'And you and I are starting a new life together. It's going to be so exciting.'

I can hardly believe any of this stuff. I just want her to be herself again. Mum's mad eyes are red, her voice is strained and tremulous. A new life with a mother as sad and exhausted as mine is right now could not be exciting.

'What do you mean?' I can't look at her and I snatch my hand away when Mum tries to clasp it again in both of hers. 'I don't want a new life. My life is exciting enough now.'

'No, but we're going to live in London and you're going to a new school. We're going to look round it on Thursday, and the term begins next Monday, so we've got lots of shopping to do. Aunt Jane's found us a flat for a while, and we will have such fun together.'

Mum croaks the last words out in a hideous attempt at cheeriness. If Mum had stood up and announced to me that she was a mermaid, or Medusa, or Lara Croft, I couldn't have been more shocked than I am now. I push my chair back and stand up.

'I'm going to watch TV,' I say without looking at her.

The children's channels all have smiling presenters who look like aliens to me, so I settle for horse racing and slump on the sofa fiddling with the volume on the remote control. I know Mum is standing outside the door – I can feel her rather than hear her – but I don't want her to come in. I wonder why Dad didn't tell me with her. I hadn't noticed I was crying, but there is a salt, wet taste in my mouth and my nose is running. I sniff, and I hear Mum draw her breath in sharply in the hall. I wish she would go away. I am too muddled and shocked to deal with her sense of guilt. The only thing I know right now is that I need to tell Nell.

*

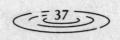

The next morning, Nell arrives early, or as early as her paper round and the bus timetable allow her to. I hear her pounding up the stairs to my room, and I can picture exactly where she is all the time I hear her until she opens the door, long red hair swinging, her cheeks pink and her eyes bright from being outside. She throws herself on to the bed next to me and through the warm cocoon of my pyjamas I can feel the crisp chill of the morning air still clinging to her as she hugs me.

'You can't really be going. She must have been kidding.'

I sit up, determined to suppress the panic, which comes in waves, and the stab of sadness I feel at seeing Nell lounging on my bed as she has done since we first became friends at primary school.

'I wish she was kidding. I keep hoping this will all turn out to be one of those nightmares like at the cinema, but so far I haven't woken up from it. We're going on Thursday to look at the school, and I start there on Monday. I can't believe that I'm not coming back with you to Flixby High. I won't even see anyone there again. I never said goodbye.'

'Why didn't they tell you before?' Nell picks up a nail file and begins sawing away at her chewed thumbnail.

'I asked them that and they both got upset. Mum said she couldn't until she knew when her job would start.'

Talking about last night, which was not like real time but more like in a 3D movie it was so surreal, is making me feel a bit more normal. I am relieved that Nell is asking me questions I can answer.

'She's going to work for a television news channel and she's really pleased about it. She said she wasn't sure if she would get it and she couldn't talk about it – I don't know. I think I believe Dad more. He just said he couldn't bear to tell me until it was real.'

'Did you really never notice that they weren't getting on?'

I have been thinking about this so much, and now I look back, I can see that the silences at home, Mum's crying, and Dad being away a lot have all added up to something so obvious, but it's amazing what you don't see if you don't want to. Nell is looking at me, her expression so kind that I crumple inside.

'No,' is all I can say.

I slump on the pink quilt next to her. She hugs me, and then places her hands on my shoulders and forces herself to smile.

'You will come back,' she says. 'You'll come to see your dad and you'll have all your London clothes and London friends and you'll be so busy we'll have to make appointments to see you.'

I shake my head, eyes blurred with tears so Nell's smile smudges into a blur with my posters and the necklaces festooned like cobwebs through the beams in my attic bedroom.

'I'll miss you, Nell.'

Nell squeezes my hands. 'Oh, Lola, I wish I was leaving boring old Flixby and starting again with you. My mum and dad have both lived all their lives here,

and I don't know how I'll ever escape it happening to me too.'

I can see myself in the mirror on the chest of drawers, my dark hair still in the plaits I did yesterday morning, before I knew. Now they are wispy and bedraggled, and my face is blotched red with crying, while my eyes are as round and sad as a cartoon of someone having a bad time.

'I'd like to stay here all my life. Or at least for now. I don't want to go with *her*.'

I can't call my mother 'Mum' right now, she has to be 'her'. And even with that distance, I still clench my jaw, because I want to scream and hit out. Why can't she go on her own to London? Dad and I could manage.

I tried suggesting it to Dad last night, when he finally appeared in the house. I know he'd been hiding from me, and he came in holding his hat in his hands and looking apologetic and agonized. He reminded me of the vicar, Reverend Horace, when he turned up at the Christies' house the other day to welcome them to the village. Reverend Horace stood on the doormat, watching Neoprene nodding to a battery-operated singing canary, and Sadie making small cakes with glitter icing, and he shifted nervously from foot to foot. Caroline made him a cup of tea, but whenever she sat down to talk to him, the telephone rang, so in the end he had to make do with me and Sadie. I was able to examine his expression closely, and Dad's was the same last night.

He shook his head when I made a perfectly good

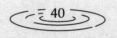

suggestion: 'I can stay with you, Dad. Please let me. I don't want to go away.'

'You need to be with your mother.'

Dad never smoked, but now he pulled out a packet of cigarettes and lit one. I gaped, astonished.

'You don't smoke.'

'No, but I am now.'

Dad's odd smirk of defiance and embarrassment stayed in my mind until I fell asleep.

'My parents have both gone mental.'

Nell and I follow the path along the creek and through the marshes towards Salt. Cactus scuttles ahead, his tail revolving madly as he sniffs in the heather for rabbits.

'My mum hasn't stopped crying for a single minute since she told me. She's supposed to be packing and starting a new life and all she can do is cry, which is useless and really annoying.'

Cactus dashes up, proudly waving a stick in his mouth. I reach down for it and throw it across a small inlet and on to the opposite bank.

'And anyway, I'm the one who should be crying because I'm being stuffed into a new school without any warning. I mean we are actually leaving the day after tomorrow—' I break off to nudge Nell. 'Look at Cactus. He's mental too.'

Wildly excited, Cactus hurls himself into the water and swims across the inlet, diagonally because of the current, yapping his enthusiasm for this brilliant game. Nell and I laugh together as Cactus leaps out and shakes himself, twirling fast to catch his tail

and nibble it before bouncing onwards in search of the stick.

'But he's mental in a dog-mental way,' says Nell. 'Not like your parents. I wonder if you will come back to stay with your dad much?'

'Of course I will, and if he's away, I'm sure the Christies will let me stay with them. Or Jack and Grandma.' I hook my thumbs into the front pockets of my jeans and walk on again, absorbed by a new thought. 'Wow, I wonder what they will say. I can't believe Mum is doing this.' And I wonder how long she has been planning in secret without thinking what she is doing to everyone else.

Jack and Grandma say nothing about Mum, although Grandma doesn't draw breath through the lunch she invites me to on my last day. Just me, not Mum or Dad or both of them, which is a bit odd. I leave our house just after midday. Dad is warming up some baked beans. Mum is upstairs packing, and I feel as though we have already left.

Grandma makes roast chicken and apple crumble, even though today is Wednesday and that is what we always have for Sunday lunch.

I keep catching her glancing at me with narrowed, anxious eyes. When it's time for me to leave, she hands me a basket containing a tin of flapjacks and three linen tea towels depicting the village church.

'Here, take this for your mother.' She looks searchingly at me. 'People never remember about tea towels when they move.' Her voice is steady; only her

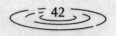

hands twisting around the basket handle reveal her distress. It is too much. I fling my arms around Grandma's neck, breathing her familiar china-tea scent, my face soothed in her soft grey jersey.

'I'll come back soon, I promise.'

'Of course you will, and I shall look forward to it.' Grandma is so calm, her eyes are bright, but she stays calm and smiling when she waves me off from her front door.

Jack walks back across the marshes to Staitheley with me. The tide is in when we reach the quay, lapping at the gangway, filling the village with the whisper of water.

'There's a bigger tide coming at the weekend,' Jack says, 'and I won't have you to measure it for me this time, will I?'

His cap is jammed down over silver-white hair, and his eyes are a paler blue than the sky. I tuck my hand in his arm.

'I bet it'll be as high as the window on that house. It's got to be this time.'

'No, not this year. We won't see another flood like that for quite a while now.'

I love Jack's flood rescue stories.

In the nineteen fifties, the water rose to the windows of Lilac Cottage where I live now. Mrs Stoddart, the doctor's widow who lived there then, had been rescued by Jack along with her three poodles, Jessica, Barbara and Anne, a set of coffee cups and her wedding dress. I drew a picture of Jack rescuing her when I was about seven, the first time Jack told me the story, and it hangs in Grandma's kitchen, next to the cat-shaped coffee pot I bought her when I was nine on a trip to London, and the three boats her boys made her when they were about the same age.

Jack stands with me on the doorstep of my house, and I look past him at the marshes. Everything feels suddenly so big and important. I am the focus of everyone's attention in the drama of my family. Suddenly all I want to do is go over to the Christies' and curl up with Sadie on the sofa.

Jack hugs me.

'It'll do you good,' he says gruffly. 'You should get away and find your own place in the world. Sometimes Staitheley is too full of ghosts and the people can be swallowed by memories. You will learn to lead your own life now.'

I hug him back, amazed, because he never talks like this. It is the first positive thing I've absorbed since Mum told me the news. I watch him turn away to walk back across the marsh, and I stay looking after him until he is a small dot, swallowed by the dusk.

Even leaving Dad, the next morning, is not as bad as it is saying goodbye to Sadie and Josh. Josh is cool. He just silently hands me a tape he has made.

'It's all sea shanties, and hymns,' he says, his voice odd and intense.

'Yes, like church,' adds Sadie, her expression angelic.

'Oh really, how nice. Ummm . . .' I am gobsmacked. Josh is into drum and bass and rap. I can't imagine where he found sea shanties. 'I can't wait to listen to them,' I add.

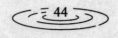

Josh suddenly bursts out laughing and picks up Sadie, swinging her around.

'You should see your face.' He grins. 'You can't have seriously thought I'd make you a tape of hymns and stuff, can you?'

'Ha ha, tricked you,' shrieks Sadie. 'It's all your favourite songs really, and I'm on it too. I sing "A sailor went to sea, sea, sea," and I did it four times to get it just right.'

3

The beeping of my phone wakes me. I read Nell's message still half asleep: *'Doing maths homework on bus. We're doing hypotenuse. Susie thought it was a kind of African piglet. Mr Riggs is a psycho. Good luck 2day. Luv Nell.'*

Outside a bus rumbles and the swish of cars passing tells me that it is raining, warm spring rain in the city, a humid experience not much like anything back at Staitheley. I sit up and tap a reply into my new phone. I have no idea about a hypotenuse.

'Tell Sooz I thought it was a vase. Wot is it? Mum got me wicked flares bx no uniform at scary new skool. Miss U XL.'

How come Nell is at school so early in the morning?

It has happened. Mum and I are living in Iverly Road in Kentish Town in North London. It takes ten minutes to walk to Camden Market and about four minutes to walk to the James Ellis Grammar School where term will begin today. Our flat is on the top floor of a big house and we face a street where buses grind and hiss and the traffic hoots and blares constantly. I have hardly seen any grass since I got to London, although there are trees covered in pink blossom in the road outside. I miss the sea, and I wish we had a house, not a flat with weird creaking sounds and the smell of the neighbours' cooking in the hallway.

The first time I walked into the flat I cried. It had nothing of home, even the smell was wrong, and being upstairs and not having downstairs makes me feel as though I have had a bit of myself amputated. Mum says she chose it because it is near school and near her office and we will move somewhere nicer when we have got settled in and she earns more. In fact, I heard her talking to her sister Jane on the phone, and I know she is waiting for the divorce to come through before she decides where to buy a flat. It sounds odd to have her talking like that – buying places to live has only ever happened for me in Monopoly. Dad and Mum lived in our house all their married life and Jack and Grandma have lived in theirs for forty years. I have never really thought about anyone moving house before; it just hasn't been part of my life. I will probably have left home by the time Mum moves. I don't know how long it takes people to get divorced, but Mum said to Jane that it took her four years to get up the courage to leave, so judging by that, I reckon I should get used to this flat with its porridge-coloured carpets and no fireplace.

The school, James Ellis, is not as bad as I thought – well, it wasn't when I went for a look round, but of course there were no pupils. Mum says it is more academic than my school in Flixby and there are nine hundred children so it is double the size. She reckons it will give me a better chance to excel. Fat chance is what I say to that, but not in front of Mum.

There are compensations for our new miniaturized version of family life. Mum has been wildly exorcizing her guilt with shopping. It is beyond amazing. When we got to London, it was like Aladdin's cave to me. I only had to say I liked something and Mum and I were on a bus heading for Oxford Street to get it. I succumb happily to the bribery, and not only because I like the stuff. Back in the flat, Mum deflates, and the red-eyed sad look returns, but out shopping she has been a real laugh, not like Nell, but differently excellent. My room is a sea of carrier bags and strewn garments, which are testament to the fun we have had. Mum has quite a good eye; she doesn't get overwhelmed by the scale of the shops, and she picks the right stuff from a rail in seconds.

Dressing for school, now on my first day, I have got as much camouflage as any girl could need, and I don't mean the army pattern. I can hide behind the newness of my clothes and no one will be able to see what I am like or who I really am.

Mum and I walk together to James Ellis. It is Mum's first day at work too, and we both burst out laughing in the hall of our little flat before we leave. Mum, small and blonde, looks like a doll in her suit, with her laptop case in one hand.

'You look like someone dressed up as a working mother.' I laugh, as she locks the door behind us. 'The only prop you haven't got is glasses. You're a cliché, Mum.'

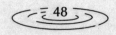

I link arms with her, suddenly aware of the two of us facing a new world together.

'I like your new stuff.'

Mum has to look up at me in my new clumpy shoes. I have never been taller than her before, and it puts her in a perfect position to notice my new dangly earrings which Nell gave me as a leaving present.

'Are you allowed earrings?' asks Mum. It is so typical of her to suddenly get all grown-up. I pull my arm away, prickling with irritation and mounting nerves as we approach the school.

'I don't know, but I wanted something to remind me I've got friends somewhere,' I snap, deliberately shifting my new school bag between us, and walking on with my head down. We are silent now, and I am looking at the clean toes of Mum's shoes, protruding into my vision with each step. Neat reminders that I am being accompanied, like a small child.

The school gates are crammed with a steady flow of pupils, jostling, walking in pairs, slowing to greet one another.

Stopping a few metres away, Mum kisses my cheek and whispers, 'Good luck.'

Still irritated, I twist my earring, and, without speaking, I step into the crowd, and immediately feel bad that I didn't say goodbye nicely to Mum.

I turn round and jump to be seen, shouting, 'Bye, Mum, bye.'

She is about to turn the corner, but she hears me and looks back, smiling and waving, standing on tip-toe to see me.

I shout, 'See you later,' and then allow myself to be swept on by the throng, and become invisible. Just moments before, I was so aware of my shoes, worn for the first time, the movement of my earrings and the rustle of fabric as my legs swung in the new flares! But now, pressed in between two taller boys carrying on a conversation over my head, and slowed by a group of girls crowded over one mobile phone, I have the oddest sensation of having vanished.

One of the boys has a handkerchief tied on his head like a pirate, and dreadlocks emerging from beneath it.

'I dunno. I've got basketball at one fifteen,' he says.

'Aw, come on, man, it's only gonna take five minutes.'

The other one reaches across me and gives the dreadlocked boy a push. They both laugh and veer off towards a single-storey block, the sixth-form hang-out.

With Mum, I spent the morning at the school last week, and although it was empty of pupils and full of the holiday smells of wet paint drying, and polish and disinfectant building up in layers, I was determined to learn my way around. Now I hardly hesitate as I go, so desperate am I not to show my newness by being lost.

My classroom is upstairs in the main building, and in it, sitting on the desks and leaning against the walls, are my new classmates. There are a lot of them, and their self-confidence radiates like heat.

'Here, dude, catch this!' a fair-haired boy yells,

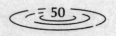

flinging something towards the door as I come in. Instinctively ducking, I just miss being hit by a rubber ball which is caught by a youth lounging behind me, a sarong wrapped over his baggy jeans. The quickest glance at him makes me feel prissy in my neat, close-fitting clothes. Shouting, 'Ready, Carl? Pete, are you awake?' he rubs the ball on his thigh and takes a short run-up like a bowler and dispatches the ball between two girls leaning on their desks to a couple of boys hunched over a phone by the window. The room is high, with big, old-fashioned windows and long rows of wooden tables. Everyone seems so at home here, wandering about, slouching to their places with envi-able confidence. For some reason they remind me of lions, or racehorses.

Hot, and horribly self-conscious, I look around for somewhere to sit. It takes every scrap of courage I possess, and the thought of my mum heading for her new job, so tiny and brave in her suit, not to turn round and walk straight out again. No one would notice, no one would know. Mum is at work. I could let myself into the flat and shut the door on this ter-rifying new prospect. It is so tempting. But before I have time to act, Mr Lascalles, our form teacher and the senior geography master, is in the room. The door has clicked shut and everyone is standing behind the desks. I slide into a space between Carl or is it Pete, and a willowy blonde girl whose expanse of deeply tanned stomach is on show, right to her hipbone, where a small pansy is tattooed. Nothing on earth could be cooler than that. I sigh to myself. How can that girl possibly inhabit the same universe as me? She can't be real. She will never, ever speak to me.

By breaktime it is clear that in the class pecking order I will be low-ranking, and the amazing girl is at the top. Jessie Tait, a sandy blonde with a down-turned mouth and freckles, is put in charge of me and is helpful, if a little detached. But nothing can alter the fact that I am new, an outsider, and I have no idea what they are talking about, so I have no way of entering any group, even if I dared speak, which I don't.

'Christoff, he's our maths teacher, is totally random,' Jessie hisses to me as we wait for Mr Christoff to arrive.

'Oh, right.' I have no idea what 'random' means in this context, so I wait to hear more.

'He confiscated Pansy's phone for no reason for the whole of last term and when she got it back all the credit was used and he totally denied it and went into a massive freak-out. He's just so rank.'

'Is Pansy the girl I was sitting next to?'

'Yeah. She's going out with Aiden Black. He's in the sixth form. He's a Rastafarian and he's the captain of the basketball team.'

I remember the boys at the gate this morning, and that one had dreadlocks.

'Does he wear a hankie on his head?'

Jessie looked at me pityingly.

'They're not hankies. They're our school colours. You know. For when you're excellent at something. He is the only one here to have got colours for basketball.' She tosses her hair back, swivelling on her

chair. 'Harry Sykes – he's in the sixth form too – has just been given them for skateboarding. It is so cool. Apparently it's the first time any school has awarded skateboarding colours, so he was in the newspapers. Everyone wants to go out with him now.' She leans confidentially towards me. 'I've snogged him in fact, but it was a year ago, so I don't think it counts any more. Do you?'

'Umm. Err, maybe,' I mutter. Ohmigod, this is terrifying, just terrifying. I have never been much of a boffin, but I am beginning to wish that there was no gap between lessons, and no time for talking ever. I mean, how obvious is it that I have never kissed a boy, let alone gone on a date? Why didn't I try to get Josh to snog me? I'm sure he would have done if we hadn't become such good friends. Oh, why did I ever go and look after Sadie and become friends with his mum? I really needed that potential experience.

Falling behind badly on the boyfriend front, I am not much better on accessories, despite my amazing shopping trips with Mum. My phone is a different make to everyone else's, which is fine, except it is much bigger – like the mobile phone equivalent of being fat. And my clothes are new in the wrong way.

'How can clothes be new in the wrong way?' Mum is incredulous. 'Surely they're new or they're not?'

I hurl myself back on the sofa, and the taut anxiety which has been holding me together all day collapses. Tears roll down my cheeks.

'Oh, Mum, you wouldn't understand. You can't just wear everything new and expect it to look – oh – there's no point in trying to tell you.'

I don't want to see the hurt look on Mum's face, and I don't want her to start telling me everything is fine, because it's not. I need to call Nell, right now. Nell understands, and goes straight to the point.

'So what did you wear?' is her first question, followed by, 'How unfriendly were they?'

Hugging the phone to my chest, I stretch out on the floor, facing the base of the sofa, my back to Mum and the room.

'Oh, Nell, it's so weird. I am not on their planet. I don't have the stuff and I haven't done anything. There's this girl in my form going out with a sixth-former.'

I stand up and go through to my room, cradling the cordless phone between neck and ear.

Nell cuts strictly through the whimpering note in my voice. 'Well, Josh is a sixth-former, isn't he? It's not that weird.'

'Yeah, but I didn't go out with Josh, did I?'

'I know that, you know that, but *they* don't, do they?'

A reluctant giggle surfaces for a moment, but dies again.

'Oh, Nell, they go out on dates and they meet in bars in the evening. No one will ever want to meet me, and there's this teacher called Mr Christoff and he sat on my hand when he was explaining something in maths to me.'

'Ooh, gross,' murmurs Nell. 'Does his breath smell? Our new geography teacher is a woman. She's called Miss Harris. Actually, she's more like a girl, really. She's only about twenty-five and all the male

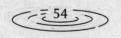

teachers follow her around with spaced-out hungry faces. It's so rank, it's unreal.'

I am restless with the phone, and now I lock myself in the bathroom and turn on the taps, partly because I want a bath, but also just in case Mum might be listening. I pour in some bath essence.

'Lola!' Nell's voice is distant. 'Are you in the loo?'

'No, I'm running a bath and it's going to be blue thanks to little Sadie's leaving present. Actually, it's a bit gross – it smells like those cartoon yoghurts Sadie likes, but anyway, I can't be bothered to let it all run out. No one will be near enough me to smell it anyway.'

Nell sighs.

'Come on, Lola, you've got to make the best of it. I think it would be brilliant to be in London. What about the shops? I'm going to fix a weekend with Mum when she'll let me come and see you. I've got to go now, I haven't done my homework and it's getting late. My mum is in a real psych. Text me tomorrow. I'm missing you.'

She is gone. I wonder whether to call back and ask how Josh is, but what is the point? I have to get on with my life in London now.

It isn't until I am in bed, drifting off to sleep enveloped in the fruit aroma of Blueberry Bubble Breeze, that I remember something awful – I haven't called Dad or Grandma, and I promised I would.

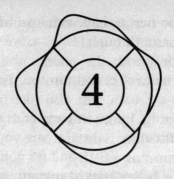

4

The first day was the worst, and, in fact, I soon become grateful for the invisibility I feel at school. It gives me the chance to get to know my way around and to work out who is who without any attention focusing on me. Jessie becomes a real friend when I notice a photograph in her locker of a terrier, and speak my thoughts out loud.

'What a nice face that dog has got.'

'That's my dog, Loopy.'

'Ooh, he's sweet. He looks like Cactus. Is he a Border terrier?'

'He's anything you want him to be. We got him from Battersea Dogs Home when he was a puppy. They found him in a dustbin with six brothers and sisters.'

I lean into the locker to look at the picture more closely; there is a dark-haired woman holding the dog in her arms.

'Is that your mum?'

'Yup.' Jessie slams the locker shut. 'She's a cow. She's left me and Dad and my sister and she's gone off with her yoga teacher. She's on holiday right now.'

Jessie's sneer hides pain I can recognize, even

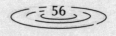

though it is too new to have made an imprint on me yet. I slide my arm through Jessie's as we walk towards the canteen for lunch.

'My parents have broken up too. That's why I'm here.'

The relief of telling someone at school brings a lump to my throat.

All my physical boundaries have changed, along with the structure of my family. I am surrounded by buildings and pavements instead of the sea. Spring bursts out all around and I scarcely notice it – I am never aware of the weather any more. I haven't once taken a coat to school; if it rains, I just run for shelter. Anyway, it doesn't matter because it isn't real rain like in Norfolk. And just as it is never really wet, it is also never really dark. Even in the middle of the night the street lamps glow orange, and I become used to sleeping through the restless city at night, only in my dreams experiencing the black silence of the nights at home.

Dad calls, and when I speak to him, I realize how odd it is not to see him every day. The funny thing is, I probably say more to him now on the phone in the evening than I did when we both lived in the same house.

'Hi, Dad, I've got history and maths homework to do tonight and I haven't even started.'

'Is it the same as you were doing at Flixby?'

'I can't really tell because everything here is done so differently. We're doing the French Revolution. I've never done that before.'

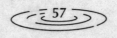

'Oh, Marat and Robespierre and what was that woman called?'

'You mean you know it?'

I am ashamed by my own surprise, but then, I've never thought about Dad in any other context than on the marshes, knowing about birds and boats and ecosystems, but not about revolutions and politics and history. Mind you, he quickly reverts.

'I think one of them was a bit of a pervert. Was it Robespierre? I can't remember, ask your teacher. When you come home, I've got lots to show you.'

'I can't ask which of the leaders of the Revolution was a pervert,' I protest. 'Tell me about Cactus, and what's happening in the village. And Grandma and Jack.'

It is May now.

Staitheley is still home. Our flat in Iverly Road is characterless and hot. I miss the familiar faces in the village, people I didn't even realize I noticed, like the milkman, or Miss Mills, or Billy Lawson's dad with his gnomic hat and his daily stroll along the quay getting slower every year with his encroaching arthritis. In London, I don't know a soul on our street, and the youth in the newspaper shop never acknowledges me with so much as a flicker of recognition, no matter how often I go in for chewing gum and phonecards.

The window in my room is stuck shut and Mum is working too hard to get it fixed, or so she says. I asked on Monday after a restless night, and then again on Tuesday and Wednesday.

'I'm sorry, darling, could you organize it yourself?' Mum says finally.

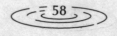

This is the last straw. I am a child, not a caretaker. I slam out of my bedroom yelling, 'Mum! Why don't you do something about this place? It's not a home, it's a cell.'

Mum looks stricken. 'I'm sorry, darling,' she repeats. 'I've been so busy at work I haven't had time to think about it.'

'Well, life isn't just about work. You've got to live somewhere as well,' I storm. 'This flat is awful. I want to go home.'

And Mum sits down on the sofa, and for once doesn't cry.

'This has not been an easy time for either of us, Lola, and I know I have neglected your needs. I am sorry for that.' God, she is so serious. All I wanted was my window open. But the look on Mum's face, which is kind of soft but strong, makes me slide down next to her. 'I don't know if I can make it up to you, but I can make an effort, with your help, to make this a happy place to be.'

'OK,' I agree. 'Let's make some rules about things each of us should do.'

The next day Mum comes back from work late with big bags of rugs and lampshades, cushions and a silver-grey velvet throw for my bed.

'Here, I bought you this because it reminded me of the sea.' She smiles, wrapping me in the silvery softness. 'And I got takeaway for supper – sushi tonight.'

Actually we have takeaway most nights. I like it. In fact I love it, although breakfast the next day isn't so great. We had curry last night, and this morning I

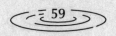

have to hold my breath, because of the rank smell of the empty cartons. I must be a very contrary person, I think, because I find myself hankering after supper at home in Staitheley when all three of us sat down together at the table for fish pie or lasagne, proper meals that I took for granted until they stopped existing.

'Why don't you cook any more, Mum?'

We are both leaning on the breakfast counter, eating cereal and watching the toaster.

'I do,' protests Mum, rinsing a mug for each of us, and throwing in a tea bag. 'It's just so nice not to do it every night, especially now I'm working, and you love takeaway, don't you?'

'Yes, but not every day.'

I pour hot water over the tea bags and pass Mum her tea. Right now I'd be happy to have breakfast with Miss Mills and her dachshund if it meant I could sit at a table with a knife and fork and have tea from a pot. Honestly, anyone who could hear my thoughts would think I am a granny myself. The truth is that Mum is happy and engrossed, and I feel left out and lopsided. Mum brought me to London and now she is getting on with her own life and I am supposed to do the same. In some ways, being treated as a grown-up is just what I want, but the contrast between now and family life in Norfolk is so extreme.

Nell is envious when she calls.

'It sounds brilliant to me to be living in a flat with no cooking or clearing up,' she says. 'We had roast chicken tonight and guess who had to peel all the potatoes, and shred the cabbage?'

'But I like cooking, and Mum used to as well,' I reply forlornly. 'We haven't had any roast dinner at all since we've been here.'

'Oh, Lola, come on. You sound like a baby,' laughs Nell. 'Tell me about the boys in your drama group. Are they fit?'

5

Sun pours through the high, smudged windows of the geography room, causing me to squint and doodle pairs of sunglasses all over my folder. Mr Lascalles is outlining a project on elements at the coast, and his enthusiasm is causing him to spit small blossoms of saliva on to the whiteboard. Unheeding of this, he continues with his marker, underlining vigorously to prove a point. The spit begins to slide slowly down the board; I shall hold my breath until Mr Lascalles wipes it off. Next to me, Pansy is pretending to write, while tapping messages into her telephone, which is hidden in a pencil case on her desktop. A buzzing begins in my head as I continue to hold my breath. Pansy's phone, which is set on silent mode, vibrates with a call.

'Cover for me,' she whispers.

'How?'

I forget to hold my breath and gulp air in. Pansy needs my help; this is a first, a chance for me to get in with her; I don't want to let her down. I must create a diversion. Pansy has draped her hair across her face like a curtain and is whispering into her phone, doubled up as if she has terrible pains in her stomach.

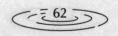

Mr Lascalles is still busy with his marker on the board, swooping his hand rhythmically like a conductor. The spitballs have gone now. Without stopping to consider what I am doing, or how I will carry it off, I stand up and move forwards.

'Sir, I wonder if you could explain this to me?'

It is like walking in the dark, but without being allowed your hands in front of you. Mr Lascalles turns in surprise.

'Dear me. I thought I was being remarkably clear,' he says.

I have no idea what I will say or do next. I bend my head over my open folder to give a studious but confused appearance. There is very little in the folder, apart from the pictures of the sunglasses. Mr Lascalles comes to stand next to me, turning his back to the class and Pansy's phone call. So that's good. My heart is pumping. Weakly, I turn the pages of my folder, hoping for a miracle.

'I'm not sure I understood our homework,' I mumble, reddening as I can feel the restless attention of the class behind me, and the heat burning in my cheeks.

This is such a lie, as the one topic in the whole of geography that I understand is the British coastline – for reasons I don't feel like telling Mr Lascalles. I gaze at him, and wish I could faint to order. I have often thought how wonderful and glamorous it would be if I was a hypersensitive person living on my nerves, always swooning and having hysterics. Right now it would be such a bonus. Mr Lascalles looks from me to my folder.

'But you haven't done it.'

Ha! I can do this one.

'That's because I didn't understand it,' I respond with a flourish.

Actually, I didn't do it because it was so easy I kept putting it off until I ran out of time. I can see a way through now. A glance over my shoulder re-assures me that Pansy has stopped talking and is leaning back in her chair filing her nails while ostentatiously chewing gum. She blows me a kiss and mouths *thank you* before turning back to her mani-cure. It has worked. Mr Lascalles is none the wiser. I didn't blow Pansy's cover; now she might even talk to me instead of looking straight through me, as she has done so far this term. The only problem now is Mr Lascalles, who thinks I am an imbecile. His face is grey and impatient.

'Look here. I think it might be better if you saw me after the lesson. We can go through it properly then.'

The bell goes. With a sinking heart I turn back to him as the others file out of the classroom.

At break I am suddenly worth talking to, and Freda, Pansy's best friend, slouches over to stand next to me as we queue for the hot-chocolate machine. It seems a good idea to loll against the radiator in the corridor with her.

'Cool belt.' Freda glances sideways at me. Pansy and a couple of other cohorts stop chewing their gum for a second, which feels like an hour. They too look at my belt. It really isn't worth all this scrutiny.

'I got it on the market,' I mutter. This is definitely the right thing to say. There is a lot of nodding, and Pansy moves to the other side of me and leans her shoulders back against the wall, her thumbs in the belt loops of her jeans.

She is so close I can smell the tutti-frutti tang of her gum mixed with some sort of musky perfume. The effect is weird – intoxicating and gross at once. I almost want to retch.

'I love the market,' she growls in the breathy voice she uses when she's really intense about something – usually Aiden. 'I'd get all my clothes there if Topshop wasn't so ridiculously cheap.'

The others nod approval, and Freda, as if revealing a huge secret, sighs, and rolls up her top to show a sludge-green vest with a small rabbit embroidered on it.

'Topshop,' she announces solemnly. 'Those big bins by the door?' Her statement is a question. Everyone, including me, nods comprehension. 'Four ninety-nine.' She makes a face, eyes big, mouth slack to denote wonder, and nodding adds, '*and* you get the knickers too.'

Everyone looks impressed. Having been about to exclaim at the shocking expense, I am forced to rearrange my expression to make it look as though I think four ninety-nine is a steal. I have a stab of anger towards my mother for never initiating me into expensive underwear. Then I think of her big old black knickers and feel guilty for being disloyal, even in my head.

Anyway, I am right in there with the girls, and for

the whole of break I am at the centre of a wide-ranging discussion about clothes and make-up. Basically, I just nod, while trying to notice every detail of movement and mannerism of Pansy's lot so I can fit in better. It is really hard work, but I manage to stand right, throwing my shoulders back, and my hips forwards. This is really good – it has the double effect of making a bit of your tummy show and your boobs look bigger. And I can do it. Everything else is so complicated. I don't know where they mean when they talk about 'Roo's' and there is a really bad moment when they talk about which drink they like best.

'I'm really into the cinnamon and orange,' says Freda, nudging Pansy. 'You were a bit off with that one, weren't you?'

'I was not.' Pansy pouts. 'Anyway, you haven't tried the black cherry. It's just coming in from the States. My dad had some from his office last week and we tried them on Saturday.' She pauses. Pansy is very theatrical and she doesn't like to miss a chance. When everyone is looking, she growls, 'It was legendary,' and we all burst into peals of laughter. I don't know quite what we are laughing at, but I need to join in.

'I really like the caramel Frappuccino,' I offer. Pansy and Freda's finely plucked eyebrows lift into their hair.

'Oh my God,' breathes Freda, 'she is unreal,' and she puts her hand over her mouth to giggle.

I have no idea what I've got wrong, but it's something. Mind you, I never expected to get anything

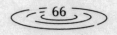

right with this lot. It's a miracle they've talked to me for the whole of one break. I shrug and turn, using the bell which has just gone as an excuse to move away. As I hoist my bag, an arm slides through mine. It is Pansy.

'Oh, Lola,' she whispers huskily. 'You are so fresh, I love it. We were talking about alcopops, not coffee shops. I'll bring you one tomorrow. But you'll have to hide it in your bag because we're under age. I promise you though, they are so lush you'll die.'

I know I'm a pushover, but I can't help finding her really endearing.

Nell is amazed.

'You mean they're actually talking to you?'

'I promise you, I am Pansy's new BF.' Delighted by having surprised Nell so much, I drop into the sofa and deliver the most impressive bit. 'She's bringing me a black cherry alcopop to school tomorrow. It's from the States. Everyone's drinking them there apparently.'

'Cool, but I bet you won't like it. You hate the taste of alcohol. Just make sure you do drink it so you can tell me exactly what it's like and I can pretend to everyone here that I've tried it too – oh. Hang on, Lola, Mum's shouting something.'

Half listening to Nell's muffled conversation with her mum, I gaze around the sitting room of the flat. I can't call it 'our' flat and definitely not 'home'. Although it is much better with the cushions and stuff. The trouble is, they are a bit like my new clothes – all bought at once to fill the space, not accumulated over time, and with love, the way things are in a home.

Mum isn't back from work. Early summer afternoon sunlight slices through the dusty window and on to my legs. I wriggle down so the warmth plays on my midriff, now permanently exposed to show I am accepted by the crowd. Mum won't be back until about seven, so I can play my music as loud as I like, or I could if I wanted to. It's funny, though, I haven't really taken advantage of the empty flat. At home I always played loud music, and I would never hear Mum yelling up the stairs at me to turn it down. The sound in my bedroom under the eaves used to swirl and fill my room – even the whole quayside if I had the windows open. Dad used to come right in and stand there smiling at himself because I wouldn't notice him and I'd carry on fiddling about, putting up posters or singing along. He never minded my music like Mum did, which is funny considering he is surrounded by quiet all day with his work. Maybe that's why.

Here, though, the silence of the flat is too enormous, and I find myself being hushed in it. I always take my shoes off when I come in; you don't need them on here, and the people downstairs might complain if they heard me clumping about in my stacks. It's weird that in the city there is no need to go outside – from getting back after school until the next morning when I go down the stairs to the street door for school again. At home, being outside was as much of life as inside, but here it hardly exists. I miss the sea. I hadn't realized how loud it was until I came away. Now all the traffic out on the road doesn't talk to me the way the sea used to, keeping me company in my room in Staitheley. Cactus would hate it here, and the people in the flat below would definitely complain about his claws skittering on the floorboards and the way he used to yap and jump in circles when I came back home. I am usually silent in the flat. The only time I shout is when I'm on the phone to Nell, because she knows just how to wind me up and make me really laugh.

She is teasing me now. I call her the minute I am back from school, and I am dying to tell her something. As usual, she goes straight to what I want to talk about.

'Hey, Lola, how's your love life now you're friends with the cool crew? It is so boring here. There is no one new to meet. And Josh is doing exams so he is always busy.'

'Actually, there is one guy.' I keep my voice casual, although I have thought of nothing else since break today. 'I've only seen him, not actually spoken to him, but this boy called Harry Sykes is gorgeous.'

'How old is he?'

'He's nearly seventeen. He's got exams so he hasn't been in school that much. He's been studying, but he's a skateboarding freak and he's a graffiti artist.'

Nell laughs. 'How can you be a graffiti artist? Aren't people who do graffiti arrested?'

'I think it's different here. He decorates the concrete bits in skateboard parks. He's been in a video of some band.'

'Wow.' Nell is lost for words for a moment. We contemplate his coolness, then she laughs again and says, 'God, can you imagine how graffiti art would go down in Staitheley?'

'Have you been to Staitheley?'

'No, but Mum was there this morning.' Nell pauses, and I know her too well for her to disguise it; she's trying to find a way to say something awkward.

'Come on, Nell, spit it out.'

My ear is hot from the phone. I can see the green clock on the music system flaring as the sun dips past the roofs across the road and suddenly the room is grey. We've been talking for twenty minutes. Mum will kill me. She says I've got to leave Norfolk behind now, because it's the only way I will come to think of this flat as my home.

'She saw your grandad, Jack.'

I don't know why my heart starts to hammer.

'But she doesn't know him.'

'I know.' Nell's voice was small, 'Oh, Lola, I think your dad should have been the one to tell you. Your grandad fell over on the quay. They were shouting for a doctor and Mum was in the fish shop and she ran out because she's a nurse. He's fine, though, he's really fine now. Mum says so and she knows.'

Cold water is flowing though me, making my heart race but paralysing everything else.

'I need to ring Grandma, Nell, I've got to go.'

'Lola, are you all right? Where is your mum, you shouldn't be on your own—'

Putting the phone down, I know I'm shaking because I miss its cradle. I have to pick it up again to

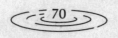

call Grandma, but I can't. I'm scared. I want Cactus to be here to hug, and my bones hurt; they're aching with loneliness. The phone rings and it is Mum. She has a sixth sense for when I desperately need her. She always knows, and it often really annoys me. Right now I really like it.

'Please come home now,' I sniff, and hot tears stop me shivering even though they are only on my face. She has spoken to Dad.

'Don't worry, Lola. He's fine. I spoke to Grandma after your father rang me. I'm coming back now, and we'll call Grandma together. Just hold on, darling, I wish you weren't there on your own.'

I don't think I'm going to cry when I speak to Grandma, but she sounds so comforting. If I shut my eyes I can believe we are in the room together.

Mum sits next to me as we talk. She can hear Grandma too, I can tell, because she is so silent, listening intently.

'Do you know, darling, I was only just back from looking for those blasted dogs of mine when they brought Jack home. He came in with a doctor beside him, and I was so surprised, I didn't know what to say, and then a cyclist arrived with the dogs.' Her voice is slower, more crackly than I have noticed before. 'It was mayhem here.'

My face is wet but I laugh when she says, 'Anyway, I've managed to get Jack to stay in bed this afternoon, and do you know, Lola, the only way I could do it was to hide his clothes. He's been listening to the racing and none of the horses he backed won. So he's very cross and I think you are the only one who

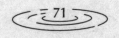

71

could cheer him up, so I'm going to get him to speak to you. Remember, my dear, he pretends to be deaf on the telephone.'

Jack says, 'When are you coming to see me?' and I look at Mum.

She holds up three fingers and mouths, 'Wednesday, Thursday, Friday and then you'll be there.'

'I'm coming for the weekend.'

'I can't wait. We'll have some fun when you get here.'

Jack sounds so jolly, I can't really worry too much now I've spoken to him. And anyway, it is so exciting to be going home, my first visit back there, and I wasn't expecting it yet because Dad's been away. But just before I go to sleep I have a fearful thought. Are they letting me go home because Jack is very ill? No one will tell me if that's the case. All I know is that he slipped over and bumped his head on the stone quay. I asked Mum if he was unconscious, but she said, 'He's going to be fine, don't worry, you'll see for yourself on Friday.' I don't know if I should believe her. I'm always the last to know. Look at the whole Mum and Dad thing.

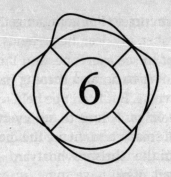

6

Dad's car radio will only work on Radio Two, so driving into Staitheley I turn off the lame country music he insists on singing along to, and open the window, craning out, this big smile slapped on my face by the warm wind and the electric excitement I feel being back. My school ended before lunchtime because all the dinner ladies in North London have gone on strike, so it's teatime and I'm home with the whole weekend ahead and Nell coming over tomorrow. My phone beeps with a message. It's from Josh.

'*Sadie says come 4 a cupcake + tea, she saw U in car just now so no escape 4 u.*'

'Dad, stop.' I am secretly relieved to put off going home. I can't quite imagine our house without Mum's presence, and I know the Christies will be just the same as usual. I also know Dad won't like it very much. 'Look, I've got to go to the Christies' for tea with Sadie. She's really excited that I'm back. Come and pick me up at five to go to Jack and Granny's.'

Dad opens his mouth to make a suggestion, but I've got my hand on the door handle and when he stops for the corner by the village shop I jump out, waving.

'Bye. Don't forget to bring Cactus, I've *got* to see him.'

'You've *got* to see everyone, and I'm waiting my turn,' Dad shouts back, and there is pain as well as teasing in his voice. But I can't be held responsible for grown-ups' feelings. I need to see everyone back in Staitheley, and small children are the most impatient. I walk through the Christies' boatyard and open the red-painted back door.

'Hell-oo, it's me, Lola,' I call, and I don't realize that I've breathed in until my senses brim with the smell of toast almost ready and tea just brewed, and the Christies' family life, with all its noise and chaos, engulfs me.

'Look, Lola, I've iced one for you and one for me. They're purple princess cakes so we're allowed to eat them first.'

Sadie charges towards me, waving two very sticky cakes, and wraps her arms around my legs. I reckon it's best to keep still, and anyway, it's a treat to hug her back. She's so small and solid but she's grown and got more of her long blonde hair falling in front of wide blue eyes since I last saw her.

'Hello there, Lola, my dear.'

Caroline crouches to remove the buns from Sadie's hands. She has funny pink slippers on over socks, tight green leggings and a baggy T-shirt. I am shocked to find myself thinking I'm glad my mum doesn't wear clothes like that. Caroline leans to kiss me, and I hug her back awkwardly. Josh's dad, Ian, appears in the doorway, also smiling, and by the time I am in the kitchen I feel exhausted by being smiled

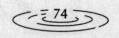

at, and under pressure of some sort because they are all so pleased to see me.

Josh, perched on the edge of a chair in front of a pile of washing, is strumming on a guitar, and is the only one who doesn't stop what he's doing to greet me.

Everything that I expected to be the same is a little bit different. Even Josh; he looks smaller, and younger, which is weird, but maybe it's because I've got used to hanging around with people like Aiden Black and he's mega compared to Josh.

Sadie tugs my arm.

'Come on, Lola, we need to play fairies to practise for when I get a loose tooth.'

And I pick her up and twirl her around, hiding my face in her neck. My feelings for her are so uncomplicated compared to everything else. When I put her down again, Josh has left the room, and the next minute he crosses the yard past the kitchen window, his skateboard under his arm. Caroline leads me to the table, chatting.

'We've all missed you, Lola. How are you getting on at your new school? Is London fun? It must seem very quiet to be back here again.'

I laugh, looking round the kitchen. A radio is perched on the window sill, mumbling away to itself, and Neoprene whistles fruitily when I catch his eye.

'Coffee and cake. Coffee and cake,' he suggests, twisting his head to one side and selecting a peanut from his bowl with one delicate claw.

Sadie has found a skipping rope and is trying to swing it in the small space between the cooker and

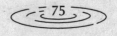

the table while chanting, 'Two-four-six-eight, who do we appreciate?'

On the cooker, a pan of potatoes is boiling, the lid clanging, steam rising and clinging to the glass panes of the window.

'No, it's not quiet here. In London I'm on my own in the flat a lot because Mum is working, but that's OK. And school isn't so bad now that I've got some friends, but it's nice to be back here again.'

I nod stupidly and push my hands deep into the back pockets of my jeans.

'I'm sure. And how is your mother finding it back in town? I expect she's meeting old friends again.'

Caroline's smile is gentle. I wish she would stop talking to me and looking at me in that very kind way she has. I just want to be with Sadie for a bit with no one paying me any attention.

'Lets play fairies outside,' I suggest. We walk down to the quay. Sadie chats for a bit then falls silent. I look down and find her staring gravely behind me.

'What are you looking at?'

'Your bum. It's waving about all over the place.'

Great. And I haven't got any other jeans with me.

When Dad comes to fetch me, I run to the car and hurl myself into the passenger seat to hug Cactus, and it is the warmest feeling I have had since I left Staitheley. He licks my face and sits on my knee, singing a long sigh. Dad doesn't talk much, but then he never did, even when I was here all the time. He

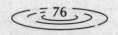

likes his own company, or that's what Mum always says about him, and I suppose it must be true.

'I hope your visit over there was everything you expected,' he says as we drive the short distance to Grandma's house.

He didn't come to the Christies' door but revved his engine and hooted his horn outside the entrance to the boatyard. Dad still looks a bit doleful, and I sat through a couple of his long silences on my way from the station, so I realize that it's best to be busy, and occupy myself by changing the settings on my phone. It suddenly shrieks (a really good sound I got for it off www.freakfone.com) and see a message from Jessie in London replying to one I sent her worrying about my bum. She is on the case.

'*4get crazy infant nonsense. Yr bum is top.*'

Mind you, she would say that because she was with me when I bought these jeans in the market. A message from a new schoolfriend who knows nothing of my life in Norfolk is weird, but I like it. As for my rear view, I'm only seeing Grandma and Jack, and Dad, so it doesn't matter if it's a bit wobbly.

The first thing I think when Grandma opens the door is that she's shrunk. The second is that the smell of her house is the best and most familiar smell in the world and I wish I could put some in a bottle and take it with me to smell when I come in from school to the flat and no one is there. It smells of clean laundry and flapjacks, pale tea and the flowery trace of the scent Grandma always wears. Oh, and a tiny whiff of the soft salt air of the marshes.

'There we are, how nice. Tike! Tansy! Get down now.' Grandma hugs me and her terriers leap to join in. 'Now you must come through and see Jack. He's been waiting for you.'

In the drawing room, Jack's usual chair in front of the fire is more inviting than ever with a pillow and a multicoloured crocheted blanket on it, and in the middle of all that, with a newspaper sliding off his lap and his glasses propped on his forehead, is Jack, looking keenly towards the door like Tike the terrier.

'Well, well,' he smiles, and holds out a hand to me.

My nose tingles and my eyes fill with tears. I'm not sure if I'm crying because I'm pleased to see him or because he looks so fragile. The copper band he always wears on his wrist is loose, but the smile in his eyes is the same as ever, and I perch on the arm of his chair until Grandma and Dad come through with a tray of tea. I don't like to say it's my second, so I don't. And it is never hard to find room for the food Grandma makes. We are all eating small sandwiches off pink china with gold stars. Tike, Tansy and Cactus are at our feet, licking their lips and looking soulful. Grandma shakes her head at them and says, 'No feeding terriers,' as if she knows I was about to split my crusts between them. Jack and Dad are discussing the recent big tides.

'There's a porpoise carcass up on the top of the island.' Dad has put his plate down and he leans back in his chair looking at the fire crackling in front of him. 'A young one. It must have got exhausted and separated from the others in the storms.'

'Unusual at this time of year,' says Jack. 'D'you know what kind?'

'No. I saw Billy and his dad today. They were collecting lugworms.'

'They never stop collecting lugworms,' jokes Jack. 'I can't think what they do with them all. The fish they're after must feast and never get caught.'

I stuff another sandwich in my mouth, as a random thought sails into my head: just imagine bringing someone like Pansy or gorgeous Harry Sykes here to Grandma's house. Imagine Harry Sykes sitting on a little low chair in his skateboarding shoes with the laces undone, eating small sandwiches off pink china. The thought makes me smile to myself, and when I go to the loo and look in the mirror, I can't really believe that I am part of both of these worlds. I look normal; well, as normal as I can with my hair out of control as usual and my eyeshadow a bit brighter than I reckoned for when I was putting it on. But I don't look like someone leading a double life, when actually that is how I feel.

I suppose it's possible that Pansy and people like her have grandparents, and maybe they even live in the country, but I can't imagine it. I am definitely the only one in my London school whose family thinks it's normal to talk about lugworms. I think I'll keep it to myself. It's better that way.

Nell is banging on the door before I have even finished breakfast the next day. Cactus leaps off my knee and quivers expectantly by the letterbox,

thinking she is delivering a news-paper. I open the door.

'You know, you even sound like a paper round person now,' I tease, as we hug each other. 'Cactus thought you were delivering something for him to eat.'

'Don't laugh,' says Nell, putting a plastic box on the table. 'But he's right. My mum has sent a batch of rolls she's made, and I don't know how old she thinks you are, but I'm afraid they're shaped like hedgehogs.'

We are both so inflated with euphoria that one peep into the Tupperware box at the shiny, brown, prickle-backed rolls with crinkled raisin eyes has us both collapsed in giggles.

'I think it's most kind of her,' says Dad, removing the lid and picking up one of the hedgehogs to admire. 'I shall take one for my lunch.'

He moves towards the chopping board with it, and as one, Nell and I shriek, 'Don't!'

'Don't what?' Dad is looking in the fridge, bringing out a few salad leaves and a heel of cheese.

'Don't cut its head off,' I plead, giggling again because I am begging for the life of a dough hedgehog.

'I wasn't going to,' he says, putting it down with its paler belly facing up. 'I was going to stuff it.'

This has me slain again, leaning on Nell, who stops laughing first and digs me in the ribs with her elbow.

'That's good,' she says encouragingly. 'Mum does that with hers when she's doing them for her wine and cheese nights and stuff.'

Dad looks very pleased to be doing the same as Nell's mum, and grates his cheese for the stuffing with a jaunty speed.

'What are you two up to today?'

And as if a connection of wires has been straining to meet and has finally made it, I feel a click and a rush of comprehension as I look at him.

He is a single parent trying to keep a relationship going with his daughter. I don't live with him and he doesn't know anything about my life now. I know too much about his life, though, because I've stepped right into the middle of it, and it isn't wonderful. In fact I feel really sad for him. It always sounded quite cosy on the phone when he called, and he told me things like, 'Cactus and I are sleeping in the arm-chair,' or 'I've been out feeding the hens and hanging my washing on the line and it's a windy day.' But now I'm here I can see that it is literally a third of the life we had when we were all here, right down to the way he orders one pint of milk from the milkman to be delivered to the doorstep each morning, when we used to have three. His washing on the line is just a couple of shirts, one towel and two big hankies. It hardly occupies one quarter of the line in our little patch of orchard at the bottom of the garden. I know, because I hung it out for him this morning. I would never have found it if I hadn't needed to wash my own stuff, and I only hung it out because I promised Grandma I would be a help to Dad, but I never imag-ined he actually needed my help. The washing had been in the machine for a while, I think. It was clean, but it had that almost mouldy smell of being left there. I wonder how long for? And the bathroom had a spider in the bath and no loo paper on the holder screwed to the wall. I cooked breakfast, but I had to go to the shop to buy bacon and butter because Dad only had bread and coffee. Dad's life is too big to take on. I prefer to think about the dough hedgehog.

'Shall I wrap it up for you?' I pull foil from the drawer where Mum kept it, and I look in the wicker basket in the larder cupboard where there always used to be crisps, and amazingly there are still some there. 'Look, here are some crisps and you can take an apple.'

Nell passes the fruit bowl, and between us we pack up Dad's lunch and wave him off. I am crying when I turn back to Nell from shutting the kitchen door behind him.

'It's hard coming back here, Nell,' I sob. 'I thought it would be just the same, but it isn't, and I feel disloyal for being relieved I don't live with Dad now, even though I can see that he needs someone around.'

Nell puts her arms round me and we stand close together in the kitchen. I am so glad she is my friend. Even thinking it makes me cry more.

'Mum says I may have to choose when the divorce comes through, and I thought I would choose to come back here, but I don't know now.'

We sit on the sofa at the end of the kitchen over-looking the quay. Our house is slightly raised, built to withstand floods, so we have a big view. Looking out at it, with Nell stroking my arm, I calm down. She is wearing a white top with hearts on it and her hair is

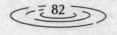

a vigorous spray of auburn from a high ponytail. She has the straightest white teeth when she smiles.

'Ohmigod!' I scream, finally noticing something that isn't directly focused on myself. 'Your braces have gone! Why didn't you tell me? When did it happen? You look so amazing. Your face is a different shape. Wow, Nell.'

Nell smiles a huge toothpaste-commercial smile.

'I wanted you to see the reality,' she says.

Now my that self-absorption has peaked and is beginning to pass, I have a thousand questions for her.

'Who are you hanging out with at school? Who has taken my place in the play? Who's going out with who?'

We would have been there all day if Dad had any food, but hunger pangs get the better of us and we go down to the shop for Pot Noodles and some sherbet dib-dabs, which Nell insists are the most lush thing ever. We are paying, and I have just thanked the third person for asking and said, 'Yes, I am enjoying life in London,' when someone touches my shoulder. I turn round, my mouth full of fizzing sherbet, and cough a cloud of it over Josh.

'Hi, Lola.' He dusts himself down and waits for me to finish coughing. 'It's nice to have you back.'

Unfortunately, I can't speak. My eyes are watering and I have to gesture to be patted on the back. Nell whacks me and I take a deep breath as we move out into the village street.

'Sorry, sorry,' I splutter. 'Yes, I know, it is weird being back . . .'

Josh is on the pavement and I am in the road, so he is towering above me.

'I suppose you think this place is just a joke now,' he mutters, and I am too surprised to say anything for a moment. He nods as though I have confirmed his thoughts. 'I knew it when I saw you in our kitchen. I told Mum you'd changed, but she wouldn't have it.'

I want to get right what I say, and I am thinking as I open my mouth to begin speaking.

'You're right, I have changed, and so have—'

The flash of anger in Josh's face is gone so fast I'm not sure I saw it, but in its place he is stony and cold.

'I'm glad you can admit it. I hope you find what you came here for,' he says, his voice so icy and polite it would have me laughing if my heart wasn't pounding in shock.

'I didn't come here for anything—' I start to say, but he has turned and is walking off, his hands deep in the pockets of his big oilskin coat, his gait clumsy but fast because he's got waders on, looking ungainly as a seal, as people dressed up for the sea always do.

'Poor Josh,' says Nell. 'He's working for his dad now, and he's thinking about dropping out of school, giving up his A levels to work full-time.' We have reached the quay, but Josh is already in his boat, untying the ropes and pulling the engine cord. 'I think the guy who worked for them had an accident and there is a big insurance claim or something. Your dad will know. But Josh is under pressure, so don't worry about it, Lola. He'll come round.'

'Why can't he finish his A levels?' The sounds of

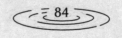

the quay, the clanging masts and the cries of gulls are so familiar they're like the voice of a family member.

'Their business can't afford them to hire an outsider so they need to use Josh,' says Nell. 'Otherwise they'll go under. My parents say this is a terrible time to be involved with the sea for your livelihood.'

Josh has his sail up now, a red triangle pulled in tight as he tacks out up the creek.

'He's had to grow up fast,' I murmur, watching him head out to sea.

All the time I am in Staitheley I have the feeling someone is watching me. It isn't a sinister feeling, it's more as if I have a person watching over me than following me in a pervy way. I don't say anything to Nell because I have been making enough of a fuss about everything already. I might be paranoid, but I think she's a bit fed up with me this weekend. I mean, I've even noticed myself that I'm behaving as if the world revolves around yours truly. Anyway, I'll make it up to her. She's got to come and stay in London at half-term. It would be so brilliant.

I'm not enjoying being on my own with Dad. It is really hard to talk about anything because Mum looms like a black hole in our conversations, and everything seems to take us towards the one subject I know we can't discuss. School, or what I am prepared to tell him about it, is exhausted pretty quickly, and we haven't even got Cactus with us to provide light relief because he would disturb the nesting terns. The only thing I am glad of is that we are outside, even though I am frozen, as I chose to wear my pale blue

T-shirt with gold writing saying 'Goddess' on it this morning. I thought about putting a hoodie over it, but I was really hoping we might bump into Josh somewhere on the way, and I had this stupid idea that if he saw me looking strong and serene and shapely in my goddess T-shirt, he would recognize how sophisticated I have become and we could meet as equals.

Of course, there has been no sign of Josh, and the lovely early summer morning has gone a bit sour. There was no way I could possibly wear the khaki jacket Dad found in the bottom of the boat when he saw my goose pimples. It smelt of diesel and it was desiccated, crumpled in a heap of salt-damp rags. It may be cold, but I am not desperate. I rub the tops of my arms and clench my teeth against the sharp air.

Occasionally Dad looks at me and shivers.

'Brrrr, I wish you'd put something on,' he says from the snug security of his classic V-neck tanktop, which I am sure was one of the main reasons for Mum leaving him. 'The sight of you makes me chilly.' He stamps and smiles and rubs his hands together as though we are approaching winter instead of mucking about on boats on a heady May day.

'Well, the sight of you makes me cringe,' I say, when he repeats his desire for me to wear more clothes for the third time. Of course, I regret it the moment the words leave my mouth. Dad kind of crumples, and he can't work out what to do with his expression for a moment. All the sadness is suddenly there, written in a headline I could not fail to read in the lines of his face, the darkness in his eyes. I feel so guilty I cannot apologize, I just heap nastiness on top of nastiness. 'We should go back. This is a bit boring and I need to pack to get back to London.' I am punishing him, but it isn't fair and it isn't helping me. I don't know how to improve things, so I go on making them worse. 'You should stop hanging on to how things were, Dad. You can't live like we're here when we're not.'

I don't even know what I'm saying. All I know is that I want to hurt him. I wish he would say something to stop me, but he slumps his shoulders and sighs.

'You're right, Lola. I have got to move on, but I'm still here and it's hard.'

Oh God. I don't want to have a heart-to-heart. In desperation I suddenly fling down my bag, take off my trainers and my trousers and scream, as if overcome by girly excitement, then race into the sea.

'Come on, let's swim!' I cry. Shit. What a mistake. 'Oh – oh. Aaah. *Oooh!*'

I am gasping, ice tingling hair, the creep of frozen flesh as my waist submerges. All the bones in the lower half of my body ache with the gnawing cold, but I plunge my head under, the water swallowing me, then spitting me out as I rear my head back, gulping, now invigorated, adrenalin racing, more alive than I have felt since I left for London.

'It's lovely, Dad. Come in!'

Admittedly, my voice is hoarse, inarticulate and breathy, but I am swimming now, striking out through the cold electric silk of the water, and energy is sparking through the choppy sea. I dive under

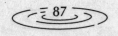

again, and it almost feels warmer to be submerged now I am used to it. The sea smells of salt and weather. You can breathe in a sense of rain to come, sun that has been glancing off the water all day. My goddess T-shirt is dark blue now, and my boobs are sticking out in a pornographic way that makes me cross my arms when I stagger out to Dad. Inevitably, he gives me the terrible tanktop, and I have no choice but to put it on. I drag my jeans over legs red and mottled like sausages left overlong in the fridge, but when I get my socks on and shake the drops of water from my hair I am glowing. I must be almost luminous, I am radiating so much well-being. And I have totally changed the mood. It was *so* worth it.

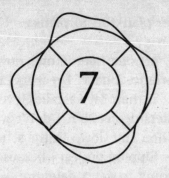

7

M r Lascalles is really bugging me. Geography has never been my favourite subject, but since half-term he's got it into his head that I need loads of support and he's always coming and talking to me about my coursework project which is mainly non-existent.

All I have managed so far is the title: 'Phosphorescence'. I am really pleased with it. I also have a brilliant photograph I found on the Internet when I looked up 'Underwater'. It's turquoise-green sea, and there is someone's mouth open like they're swimming, but its blurred so it looks as though they are deep underwater. I spent hours in the IT room printing it and touching it up and I've stuck it on the cover and written 'Phosphorescence' over it in silver. I think it looks great; so do Pansy and Jessie and everyone, but Mr Lascalles keeps going on about content. No one else has a photograph on theirs, and at the end of the last lesson he muttered something about it not being in the brief. I pretended not to hear. But today, he suddenly decided that the project is meant to be about sea defences, when I *know* he just said the sea or maybe the coast last week. I am quite unkeen to change from plankton to planks – I just can't be bothered.

Of course, no one here knows how much first-hand sea experience I have. I reckon I must know a lot more about it than Mr Lascalles, even though he has got a Masters degree, but I don't want to boast. And in fact, when I sit down in the school library to finally start my flipping project – because if I don't do it today I'm going to get a detention – I find that I can't actually think of one single tiny thing to say. It is so horrible being stuck in a library for a whole lesson when you have nothing to write.

First, I draw a few mermaids on the back of my folder, then I shut my eyes in the hope that some thoughts will flow into my brain. I think I must have fallen asleep, because the next thing I know is that I've got pins and needles in my arm, and my face, propped on my hand, is hot and numb. For an awful moment I think I might have dribbled, but luckily not. Jessie is getting going with her project at the next computer. I flick a paper pellet at her and she turns round.

'You were out cold,' she mouths. 'What have you written so far?'

'Nothing,' I mouth back.

'Try the Internet,' she urges, and idly I type in the word 'Phosphorescence'.

This small act changes my life.

What a nightmare. It is so bad. Who would have thought it? From being about to get detention for my lack of project, I have been catapulted to teacher's

pet. Not Mr Lascalles's pet though. He said my project was fanciful and absurd, and I was all set to get a C and forget about it when it was just my bad luck that Mrs Bailey, the Director of Studies, decided she was going to read some of my work to see how I was getting on.

Of course she chose the geography project, and, weirdly, she *loves* it. She says I have a gift for creative writing. Mr Lascalles snarls when I tell him this.

'You're not supposed to write creatively in geography.' He slams his fist on my folder. 'Where are your facts, Lola?'

Search me. My main worry now is Mrs Bailey and her enthusiasm. She is out of control and tells everyone that I am a gifted child. Let me tell you, I am *not* gifted, nor do I want to be. Worse still, she has decided that she is going to read out some of the project in assembly next week. Not all of it, thank God, but the beginning. Little does she know that it is a patchwork of deceit, made up of things I found on the Internet, combined with some of my dad's reports on the birdlife at home. I quite often just substituted the word 'plankton' for 'tern', as in 'The migrating plankton return to our shores in April.' It looks good, and evidently Mrs Bailey doesn't know any more about birds or even plankton than I do.

'You are to be congratulated, Lola. You have found a way of expressing yourself that will speak to all of your classmates,' she enthuses, and I can only bear to look at her face for a moment because her mouth is wobbling with excitement and her chin

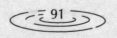

seems to move freely from side to side beneath it without seeming to be attached to her jaw.

Mrs Bailey is the kind of teacher that you recognize by her smell and remember for the whole of your life. My first primary school teacher had the same thing – she was called Miss Lord and she smelt of some really nice soap. Mrs Bailey is more essence of violets or some such delicate flower, but the scent is distinctive, and nothing will ever stop me thinking of her when I smell it.

Mum is thrilled for me when I tell her the awful news about my project.

'That is great, Lola,' she says, looking up from her newspaper for once.

She is sitting across from me, with her feet curled up under her on her chair. We are quite like a married couple from a sitcom in the way we have a routine for our lives. I love routine. It is such a relief after the chaos of moving and everything. I have always responded to routine; I often think it is because I lived by the sea, and the tide is the world's oldest routine, I guess – after the cycle of the moon and the sun.

Anyway, I usually do my homework before Mum comes back from the office. We cook dinner together, or rather, Mum cooks and I start to help, but then I have to go and put some music on, or call Nell or something, and by the time I come back Mum has made supper. Quite often it's stir-fry with cashew nuts, which I love. I would lay the table if we had one, but we don't. We have TV dinner, which is fine when there is something to watch.

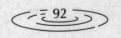

It was really gross a few days ago, though, because they had a programme about plastic surgery on when we were eating. It is so mental to be cutting up chicken breast and posting it into your mouth while watching a surgeon slice into a woman's face and take out bits that look like meat from her cheeks. It made me want to be a vegetarian for about an hour or two. Anyway, I'm not a vegetarian, but I'm thinking about giving up red meat. Quite easy, as we never eat it anyway. Even easier to give up fish, actually, as I don't much like it, and I can say so now we don't live by the sea any more.

'To have your project read out at school is so impressive.' Mum pushes her hand back through her hair and her silver bangles clank.

'But it's not because it's good,' I have to point out. 'It's not accurate or anything. In fact the geography teacher said it was a load of old rubbish.'

'That was unnecessarily rude of him.' Mum has a purposeful look on her face, as if she might threaten to come into school.

'No – I mean the thing is that the Director of Studies *likes* the way it's written, so never mind Mr Lascalles. He is so yesterday with his views.' I stumble over the words to get them out in time to mollify Mum. It works.

'Well, I'm glad you have a strong voice already,' she says.

Mum looks completely different now we have left Dad. She has had a haircut, and they gave her a fringe, which secretly I think was a mistake, but also I do think that she looks quite young, which is good,

I suppose. She has also started wearing a lot more make-up, which actually makes her look a little older. The combination of the young hair and the old cosmetics leave her about where she was before, but groomed and polished instead of careworn and miserable. Her clothes are better too, and she wears skirts all the time.

'I never want to see an oilskin garment again,' she said when we were packing to move. And it is as though she has completely turned her back on the life we had in Norfolk. Mum never even looks out of the window, never mind goes outside. She just floats around wearing glossy tights and heels and silky skirts with little tops. I feel galumphing and huge next to her, because she seems so small and slight. It's as if the shabby outer casing of her when she wore big jumpers and had manky-looking hair has been shaved off, and inside is a shiny new little jewel-like mum.

'So, is it being read out for its literary merit or because it's a good project?' she asks.

Sighing, I zap the TV silent and continue to stare at the screen.

'Not sure.'

A man with purple sunglasses opens and closes his mouth like a goldfish. Losing the sound has always been the best way to watch bad music acts.

'Actually, Mum, I'm not so keen on the geography project being read out at all.' I prefer not to look Mum in the eye when I am disagreeing with her, even if the disagreement is only tiny, like now. 'It will make me feel a bit of an idiot to hear what I wrote,

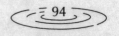

and I hate the idea of everyone else knowing it. It's like being naked or exposing myself or something.'

Mum laughs, another new form of expression for her, and I zap the sound back up because the bad song has finished and the next band on are quite good. Mum doesn't seem very bothered by anything I do. She hardly ever tells me off, and she's more likely to laugh if I do something wrong. It's weird. Come to think of it, she doesn't often ask me about my day, or what I had for lunch, but I tell her anyway, because after all the years of her asking me, 'How was school?' it is automatic to give her an edited version of my life.

I almost did it when I got back from the weekend with Dad, but I saw a barrier go down behind her eyes, so I stopped myself and said, 'Oh, well, you know, it was just like it always is there. Nothing happening to no one.'

Mum smiled, gratefully I think. She said, 'I'm glad Jack's recovering.' But actually she didn't sound any more glad than she would have been if someone on *EastEnders* was getting better from an illness. Now she lets the subject of my project drop and goes back to tapping information into her Palm Pilot. She reminds me of a nine-year-old kid on a PlayStation.

Nell and I discuss her, late at night when I am in bed with the duvet over my head and the phone sneaked from its cradle in the sitting room while Mum is having a bath. She has now had enough of my extended conversations and is beginning to be a real pain about the phone bill.

'I didn't ask to move to London away from my

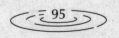

life and my friends,' I pointed out to her, when she started psyching out just because she couldn't get through trying to ring me from work for a measly half-hour. That shut her up for a while, but tonight I want to keep things simple, so Nell and I talk quietly, and I absolutely won't be on the phone for hours.

'You know what, Nell?'

'What?' Nell yawns. She is in bed too, but not hiding because she doesn't need to. I was the one who called, and anyway, Nell's mum hardly ever gets in a psych. She's really cool.

'I think my mum is in love.'

'Is she?' Nell's surprise makes my toes curl up and something shrivel in my stomach.

I'm only fourteen. I shouldn't have to deal with my mother being in love.

'Well, she laughs a lot, she doesn't eat much any more. She looks amazing and she isn't at all interested in me.'

'I don't think that's love,' says Nell. 'In fact it sounds like the opposite. Most people in love look ghostly and are always hanging around the phone. Does she do that?'

I think for a minute and realize I have hardly ever given Mum a chance to be on the phone because I am always using it.

'Er, no,' I concede, cautiously.

'Sounds as if she's happy,' says Nell. 'It would be a bit weird of her to fall in love so fast. You've only been in London six weeks.'

'Yes, but maybe she already knew the person and that's why she left Dad.'

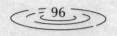

As I speak these words I realize that this has been the shadowy thought in the back of my mind all along. Saying it is a relief, particularly when Nell laughs down the phone.

'Don't be daft. How was she ever going to have met some swanky London person when she never went anywhere? Your mum never left Staitheley. My mum says that was the problem. She didn't have enough to do and she got bored. Now she's busy and she's happy. End of story.'

'I know . . .' There is a click as the bathroom door opens. 'Sh for a minute,' I whisper, holding my breath. There is a waft of scented air as Mum comes out of the bathroom. She pauses by my door and then a moment later I hear her own door creak and close. 'Are you still there, Nell?' I whisper.

'Yeah, I'm going to have to go in a second, but I've got to tell you – you'll never guess – Josh is going out with Fay Bullock. They were snogging at the sixth-form disco. D'you remember her? She's got huge tits and a kind of flat face.'

Oddly, it is not the nature of the information Nell is passing on that freaks me out, it is the way she obtained it.

My heart is thudding as I ask, 'How do you know? You weren't there. Year Tens aren't allowed to go to the sixth-form disco unaccompanied.'

Nell answers hesitantly, 'Well, I was there actually. And I wasn't unaccompanied. I went with Jason Dawes.'

'Oh *my God*, you—'

The door spins open and Mum is there in the

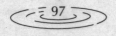

block of light from the landing, doing her most icy, no-nonsense whisper.

'Give me the telephone.'

Mum holds her hand out and I pass the phone like a small and unsuccessful relay baton.

I can't bear it. Nell had a date, she went to the dance with a sixth-former, she *must* have kissed him in the slow dance at the end, and now I am the only person left of my age who hasn't done proper snogging. Or ever been out with someone. The evils of the geography project are nothing to this.

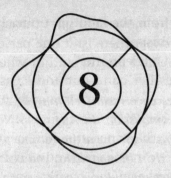

8

Assembly is a big deal at my school. It doesn't happen every day, but when it does happen, everyone has to go, and there is a register on the way in to make sure we are all there. Sometimes we have a guest speaker, sometimes a class takes over and runs the show. It is always too hot, and the floor smells of polish and shines and squeaks beneath your shoes.

Assembly is most boring when the usual members of staff are doing the usual thing of leading the prayers and talking, so on the day that Mrs Bailey stands on the platform with my project, everyone is glazed over with the tedium of it all when she gets up to speak. She puts on her glasses, stuffs one hand in the pocket of her sensible long cardigan and coughs, looking over her glasses at the rows of pupils.

'This morning I am going to read to you from one student's work. I have chosen this opening part of a project because it displays energy and clarity, it is poetic and lyrical, and because it opens a door in the imagination. The pupil who wrote this is in Year Ten.'

Oh no. My face, burning since she started waffling, bursts into clammy perspiration and everyone in my year group turns to look at me. The

whisper and the movement goes through the whole school, and I swear there isn't one person there who doesn't know that I am the author when Mrs Bailey begins to read.

'*Phosphorescence means shining in the dark; luminous without combustion. In August in Norfolk, the sea warms to a point where the algae become phosphorescent. If you swim at night in moonlight, you become luminous, the water droplets around you sparkle green fire, your skin drips light like sequins, and you seem to be made of glittering scales.*' Mrs Bailey pauses and looks around at all of us. There is an ungodly silence which makes me want to faint, if only I bloody could. She carries on. '*You are a mermaid when you swim in phosphorescence. And you glow in the dark.*'

There is a small silence as she finishes, then a shimmering giggle which starts at the front and surges back through the room.

Surely she could have left that bit out? It is so unmerciful, so blistering to read out something that was never meant to be heard by anyone. Mr Lascalles seems to be the only person who shares my view. On the platform behind Mrs Bailey he is sitting sideways on a chair, one hand over his eyes as he shakes his head.

I hadn't thought much about what it would be like after the project was read out, and if I had, I would have imagined even more people avoiding me than normal and a lot of sniggering. But what actually happens is really surprising. I am on my way back from the science block after physics, texting Dad to tell him about substituting terns for plankton. A group comes towards me on the covered walkway and, without looking up from my phone, I pause to let them pass.

'Hey.' There is a scuffle of feet as the group stops next to me, galumphing a bit like the elephants in the *Jungle Book* cartoon. Harry Sykes, whom I have never spoken to before, but who is still the fittest boy in the school in my view, is grinning at me. My hands become solid lumps, nerveless, and I drop my phone. He picks it up and hands it back to me.

'It was your stuff in assembly, wasn't it?' His eyes are blue and his hair is the colour of wet sand, but I can't stop looking at his mouth, his teeth white and straight in his smile.

'Yes,' I croak.

Not even Jessie knows I have had my eye on Harry. Only Nell, safely in Norfolk, has heard about him from me. It is one of those secret situations, so enjoyable to hold to oneself because to release it would make everyone laugh. Harry Sykes is more of a god than Aiden and all those superstars in the basketball team; the graffiti art for the rap band he did last holidays has been seen on television, and the fact that he comes to school is generally considered by fellow pupils to be more him doing the James Ellis Grammar School a favour than them giving him an education. It is ridiculous to try and explain how cool he is and here he is talking to me.

'How do you spell "phosphorescence"?' he asks. 'It's a wicked word. I want to look it up online. I like

the whole deal about the plankton and the luminosity. Have you actually ever seen it?'

I almost rise off the ground with amazement because he appears so impressed when I answer, 'Oh yeah, I've seen it; I've swum in it, and I will again this summer I should think.'

To have Harry Sykes of all people looking at me with proper focus and a bit of awe is too much. I am not ready for this.

He steps closer and leans one hand high on the wall behind me so he is less than an arm's length away, and he says, 'Can you show us it?'

I am poleaxed by the notion of Harry Sykes and his gang splashing about in the sea looking for phosphorescence. My small patina of sophistication deserts me, and mouthing like a goldfish is all I can do until another weird thing happens.

Mr Lascalles approaches and, instead of rushing past with his head down, creases his face into a smile and says, 'Lola, I was looking for you. Your project has triggered a thought.'

Why does he have to come and talk to me now? There will be thousands more opportunities, including our sodding geography lesson, but right now, in front of Harry Sykes and his mates, is just the worst. My eyes dart between Mr Lascalles and Harry. I don't know how to keep them both chatting, and in fact I wish the ground would swallow me.

'Has it?' I mumble, not looking him in the eye and trying to twitch my face into an expression that is both attentive to Harry and off-putting but not rude to Mr Lascalles.

'Yes.' He barks a loose cough. Harry raises his eyebrows and waits. Mr Lascalles pulls out a large red handkerchief. 'I'd like to take a group to the Norfolk coast for a camping trip. I wonder if you know anyone there who could give advice on the logistics?'

Undoubtedly I should answer 'No', but I am still intoxicated by Harry Sykes and his interest. So I nod like a hypnotized sheep, and bleat, 'Yes, I know just the person. He's my dad actually. His name is Richard Jordan and he's the warden of the North Norfolk Heritage Trust.'

'Warden sounds like jail to me, sir.' Harry's expression is grave; his friends have sceptical expressions on their faces. Mr Lascalles is polishing his glasses.

I can't forget that he blew his nose on that handkerchief just a moment ago. I shake my head.

'No, not that kind of warden. He looks after the land and the wildlife, he—'

Even Mr Lascalles snorts with laughter. They are all taking the mickey out of me and they are the ones who want to go to Norfolk. Hot tears smart in my eyes. I have to get away.

'I'll put his address and stuff in your pigeonhole, sir,' I call, walking away fast towards the canteen. That's the end of my one and only conversation with Harry Sykes.

'It will really surprise me if anything comes of this,' is my thought as I put my dad's work address and his mobile number in the box marked 'Lascalles' the next morning. Everything slumps back to normal

after that, except that I keep glimpsing Harry Sykes whenever I am walking between lessons. Sometimes he waves, sometimes he just nods, but he doesn't come and talk to me again. Thumbing through an old biology textbook, I notice his name on the flyleaf. He has done it in a kind of 3D writing and I run my finger across the page, imagining him labouring over it for hours, although I reckon he's so good that he probably designed this in about two minutes flat. In a weird way, I feel more isolated now than I did at the beginning of term. Then I was properly invisible because nobody knew me, but now, what with my crush on Harry eclipsing any other interests I might have had, I don't want to hang out with Jessie because I don't want to tell her about it, especially as I remember her telling me she once snogged him. Even though it was ages ago, she may still fancy him. Pansy and her gang have given up on me because I am seen as a swot since the assembly reading.

Nell is the only person I can talk to about it, but I know the gap is widening between us. She is now going out with Jason Dawes, and even though she does her best to make light of it, I am left behind. We have one brief text chat.

'Wot's snoggin' like?'

'Like havin' a goldfish in your mouth.'

'How do U do it?'

'U try and stick your tongue as far as U can down their throats. They like that.'

'Do U like it?'

'Not really, actually, it's OK. Don't all the girls at your school do it?'

'Probably.'

We used to go through every new experience together, but it isn't possible any more. Nell's parents aren't divorcing, and I am finding my way among a new group. I feel a long way from home.

There is a party next weekend. Pansy and Freda have invited most of the girls in our year and most of the boys in the sixth form. For some reason they have also asked Dave Fisher, a real drip who has got a crush on me. He has asked me to go with him, but I am hedging. Actually, I don't much want to go at all. It is a terrifying prospect, a party full of older boys, drink and no parents around. I've never been to anything like that, and I know Mum wouldn't let me if she knew.

'This looks fun. I'm glad you're making new friends,' was all she said when she saw the invitation.

It's true. From the glossy green of the apple on the front of the invitation, and the gingham design of the lettering, you get an impression of wholesomeness which is obviously designed to mislead any suspicious parents.

'My sister's getting us a case of vodka alcopops from the place her boyfriend works.'

Freda is trying to encourage a group of boys in the lunch queue behind us with the lure of alcohol.

'Oh, right,' says one of the boys she has addressed, as he reaches past her for a plate of pasta. His name is Vince, according to the embroidered pocket on his bowling shirt. I don't know why she is

so desperate for him to come, as he and his friends spend their whole time in the skateboard park up the road and only seem to come to school for lunch. Sometimes I really know I am on a different planet from the rest of my class.

Three days before the party I have the hugest spot in the history of humankind on my nose.

'What spot?' says Mum when I charge into her bedroom to ask for something to cover it up.

'*Mu*-um,' I wail. 'Please don't pretend you can't see it.'

Mum is drying her hair. Her room is warm and bright with the radio on and the window open to let in the scent of the blossom tree which is in flower in the garden behind our flat.

Her room is much quieter than mine. I never open my window. I got used to it when it was jammed shut, and even now it's mended, I don't bother; it seems pointless because the street below is so loud and dirty. Mum turns off the hairdryer and goes to her dressing table where she pulls open a drawer.

'Here, try this. It is hardly noticeable – I promise.' She dabs something on my nose and looks at me, right up close so I am reflected in her eyes. It's funny how if you look at a pair of eyes on their own without taking in the whole face, they could be anyone's. Mum's are so clear and brown, with the whites

almost blue, that you would think they were a child's
eyes. Then she smiles and her pupils blur as she
comes and kisses me. 'You'll be fine, no one will
notice, and—' She is interrupted by the phone
ringing. She answers it.

Her face tightens.

'Oh, hello.'

Pause.

'Yes, I see. You must talk to her yourself.'

I know it must be Dad.

'Lola, darling—'

Dad doesn't call me darling, so that's odd for a
start. Somehow I don't want to hear what he is about
to say, so I rush on, which is what I always do with
Dad if I can.

'Hi, Dad, Did you get my message about the
terns?'

'Yes, but—'

'I've got to go to school now, you know.' I have
to pause, because it is time to go, and I haven't let
him say what he was going to. He coughs and continues, talking over me.

'I thought I'd better ring before you left. I wanted
to see if you could change your plans and come home
this weekend instead of next?'

This is the excuse I need not to go to the party,
but now I have it I'm not so sure I want it.

'Why? I've been asked to a party in London this
weekend, and I've been really looking forward to it.'
God, I am such a liar. I didn't want to go at all until
this moment. 'And I've made loads of plans for next
weekend in Norfolk with Nell and people. And I'm

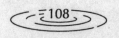

going to help Grandma with Jack's birthday. That's why we set it for next weekend, Dad.'

Mum is rolling her eyes and looking at her watch. Dad sounds exasperated.

'Well, I think Grandma and Jack would like you to come this weekend instead now. He's had another fall and the doctor thinks it's a minor stroke. Seeing you cheers him up so much.'

Sometimes I really wish I wasn't an only child. I hate being the only one who cheers everyone up. It's such a responsibility. It makes me heartless.

Mum is waving her keys.

'I'll see. I'll call you later.'

I put the phone down with a crash and grab my homework.

'What shall I do, Mum?'

We are on the way to school, and Mum is marching along at such a rate I have to jog to keep up. We are overtaking everyone else walking along the pavement. I should have worn my cheesecloth top because although it's still cool enough for goose pimples in the shade of the high wall, out in the sunshine it's hot and so bright you blink.

'They said today would be a scorcher,' she says, slowing down but not stopping as she twists her hair up on her head and clips it with a tortoiseshell claw.

'Should I go up and see Jack and Grandma this weekend? But then I'll miss the party, and I'll have to go *again* the next weekend because I can't miss Jack's birthday. Oh, it's so annoying. And I haven't got any suncream and I'm going to fry.'

The school gates loom. Mum passes me a fiver.

'Here's some lunch money. Stay in the shade and drink water. You have to decide yourself what to do. I can't make your decisions for you.'

I knew she would say that, and it doesn't help one little bit. Hot and cross, my spot pulsing like a heartbeat, I head for my class.

By lunchtime I have a bad headache and no friends. Well, that might be a bit dramatic, but it's how I feel. I think some of the girls in my year are looking on the party as a chance to do everything. No stopping at anything. I've got Dave Fisher as a date, although I haven't actually agreed to go with him yet, and I've never snogged anyone at all. I definitely don't want him to be the first. It couldn't be worse. I may as well go to Norfolk and stay with Dad, as nothing could be more humiliating than the party.

I take myself off to the proper-meals window of the canteen when all the others go for sandwiches because I need to be on my own.

'OK, dallin'. Whaddyahavin', dallin'? Come on, come on.'

Esther, the Filipina dinner lady, beams at me and waves a giant ladle over the possibilities.

Everything looks rank. I point at the last portion of tuna salad, the least wilted-looking plate on the stainless-steel worktop.

'Toonatoonatoona,' she bellows back into the kitchen behind her. 'We need more-an'-more-an'-more.'

I am sitting in the shade on my own, fanning myself with the polystyrene tray from my food and trying to wipe a blob of mayonnaise off my T-shirt

when Harry Sykes drops out of the air and lands cross-legged next to me. Well, I'm sure he just walks up and sits down, but it *seems* that he drops out of the air.

'Will you come with me to this party on Saturday?'

He is twizzling a pen round his fingers. It flashes in the sunlight and I gaze at it, not him, and remain speechless. I am thinking, 'Thank God I didn't tell Dad I'd go home this weekend.'

'I could come round to your house and pick you up, or we could meet at the skateboard park.'

Harry obviously thinks silence means yes. He lies back in the grass next to me with his hands behind his head and closes his eyes. I can't look at him. I can't look anywhere except at the grease mark on my T-shirt.

I don't know what would have happened, or how I would have managed to move again, if Jessie hadn't come over, wiping her hands on her skirt and kneeling down on the grass next to me.

'Sykes, what are you doing?' It is a surprise to me that anyone can address Harry Sykes in anything less than an exultant whisper, but I have to remember that not everyone sees him as a deity. So when he opens his eyes and grins at Jessie, saying, 'I'm asking your friend Lola to come with me to the party,' Jessie just says, 'Oh, right.' She gives me a speculative smirk and a wink before standing up.

'I'll leave you to it then.'

She moves off towards another group.

I must say something. I cough to clear my throat which doesn't work so I croak, 'I'll meet you at the skateboard park.'

Harry looks pleased. He holds out his hand flat, and I put mine in his, as solemnly as if we are exchanging vows. Harry pulls the lid off his pen with his teeth and bends over my hand, writing something.

I burst into slightly hysterical laughter.

'It tickles so much,' I protest.

'I've finished.' He stands up without letting go of me, so I am pulled to my feet as well.

'To remind you.' Harry picks up his folders. 'See you later.'

He dodges a basketball which has just bounced out of the court, and wanders away.

I look down at my hand. He has drawn a wave with droplets making the letters of my name and a tiny dog just above my wrist-bone.

Pansy and Freda pass as I am gazing in wonder at the back of my hand.

'Ooh! Harry's tagged Lola,' calls Freda in a voice dripping with innuendo. I smile at her, revelling in what is definitely my best moment at the school so far.

'It's good, isn't it?'

My voice is laid-back and cool. This sensation is beyond. Beyond everything.

Suddenly everything has changed in school, and I can hardly wait to get there in the morning because Harry is waiting for me at the gates. Mum has gone on an assignment to Paris. She warned me it might happen, and she said a friend of hers would come and look after me, but I wasn't paying attention. So Ali

arrives, and I am gobsmacked. Ali is a macrobiotic. She does a lot of chanting and meditation and hates Radio One. We get off to a bad start over breakfast. I am eating cereal and reading the packet when Ali suddenly snatches the box and chucks it in the bin.

'What are you doing?'

I am astonished and freaked out.

'You must boycott this company,' she urges, her eyes bulging madly. 'They are destroying Africa with their cynical exploitation of workers.'

My Coco Krisps don't taste quite the same, but I try to eat them.

I would normally be desperate to get away to Staitheley rather than eat bean sprouts and boycott cereal but I am so pleased about the timing of her stay. Ali doesn't have a clue what I'm doing or ask me about my homework and stop me talking on the phone, and she doesn't walk me to school. Mum would notice how distracted I am, but Ali doesn't know any better. The moment I dread is the moment when I can no longer put off ringing Dad. I psych myself up to do it just before I am due to go shopping for a skirt with Jessie. That way there is a treat after the horror.

'I'm not coming this weekend, Dad, I'm afraid. But I'll be there for Jack's birthday as we planned.' There is such a long silence I think he must have been cut off. 'Dad? Are you there?'

'Yes, I heard you, Lola, I heard you.'

He sounds so tired, and so despondent, I just want to get off the phone. I can't deal with it.

'I've got loads to do this weekend, Dad, sorry.'

Even as I'm saying sorry I'm actually feeling angry. Dad is such a one for making you feel bad, and now, whenever he rings up, I seem to feel bad, and I don't want to go back to Staitheley and see him, and that makes me feel worse. 'I've got to go now, someone's at the door.'

Mum sends a postcard from Paris. It is of a cabbage, and she's written it in French. Not my best subject, but it looks quite interesting. I have to wait to get to school to decipher it with a dictionary: '*Mon petit chou*,' she has written. '*N'oublie pas le linge et aide Ali avec la vaisselle. Gros bisous, ta mère.*'

I find out that '*le linge*' is not lingerie, as I had hoped, and therefore not a lovely present for me from Paris, but is bloody laundry so that means that '*vaisselle*' isn't worth looking up, because it is bound to be slaving of some sort.

I am in the library with the vile Miss Blessup. She has a couple of girls from my year helping her clean out the hamsters, who are called Cake and Bread. Verity and Sarah are such operators. You get off library duty early for cleaning out the cage. I wish I hadn't wasted my time translating that postcard, it's just made me cross.

My bad mood lasts until I begin getting ready for the party with Jessie. We decide to start about two hours early, and Jessie comes to the flat with her clothes in a plastic bag. She immediately makes herself at home in my room, plugging in her heated curling tongs, putting on a CD she has brought to create an ambient atmosphere, and kicking off her shoes.

'It's always better to get ready with someone else,' she pronounces, leaning on her elbows in front of my mirror and applying a smear of my purple shimmering eyeshadow to her eyelids.

I nod, wondering if I dare ask her what it was like to snog Harry. She pre-empts me.

'Have you snogged Harry yet?'

I shake my head. She gives me a knowing smile. 'Well, you will tonight, so make sure you brush your teeth.'

Oh God. I am in the bathroom, cheeks burning, brushing my teeth like there is no tomorrow. I have brushed pink hair mascara all over my fringe and I look as if I have trailed my head in icing. Oh, well. It is a miracle that we aren't late when we finally leave the flat, although I have to walk in a foolish fashion with my mouth half open and my hands dangling in front of me. I don't want to close my mouth in case my bubblegum-flavoured lipgloss rubs off before I meet Harry, and my hands are flapping in the breeze to let my neon-green nail polish dry. Jessie can't stop giggling because just before we came out we noticed that the name of the nail polish is 'Snot Snog'.

'How can they think anyone will buy something called Snot Snog?' she wails, getting the bottle of polish out of her bag as we walk through the balmy May evening towards the skateboard park.

'Well, we did,' I point out to her. 'And we didn't stop to look at the name. D'you think we might not have bought it if we'd known what it was called?'

The air is full of scents – flowers, almonds from the Spanish grocer's shop on the corner, a rush of tobacco from the boys waiting at the bus stop, all laced with fuel from a lorry hissing its brakes at the traffic lights and the acrid smell of warm tarmac.

I have been feeling guilty about not going to see Dad since he called, but, as the traffic lights change and the lorry grunts away, I catch sight of Jessie and me in a shop window. We look so eager, waiting to cross the road, both wearing new tops and a bit more make-up than we really meant to. My bad mood and my nerves vanish, and I can tell I'm going to have a good time tonight.

Harry is waiting at the skateboard park, lounging against the fence. He walks towards us, and the lazy, teasing smile on his face is probably the sexiest thing I have ever seen.

'You look great,' he says. 'I like your pink hair.'

I laugh, and blush. I am no good with compliments, I don't know where to look.

'I've got some alcoholic lollipops,' Jessie suddenly announces, cutting through my embarrassment brilliantly. 'They came in some promotional thing my dad got and he gave them to me. They're supposed to be gin-and-tonic-flavoured.'

'They're bound to be really disgusting,' says Harry, contemplating the green lollipop. 'But let's give them a go.'

The party is down some steps in a mews next to a restaurant. People are spilling out of the door, smoking self-consciously, and the bass line of the music thuds through me, as much a sensation as a sound, as

we queue to go in. I am glad me and Jessie are with Harry when we have to give our names at the door. A man in a black T-shirt draws a Day-Glo cross on my hand and we go into the party.

It is the most unrelaxing experience of my life. Everyone is looking at everyone else, but mostly without speaking. I am still holding my lollipop, and I become obsessed with trying to put it down without being seen. In the end I drop it on the floor just as Freda and Pansy walk past. Pansy treads on it, but doesn't notice it sticking to the heel of her shoe. Nor does she see me and Jessie, standing right behind her. Bronzed and made-up, she and Freda have tried hard, and they are golden and glorious to behold. They look like goddesses from a Greek myth, particularly as both of them have strapless tops on and their shoulders glitter with body paint when they move.

'Pansy looks like she's come as her own going-home present,' Harry whispers in my ear, then adds more loudly, 'She should have a label on saying "Fool's Gold" to protect people who know nothing about her, or the fact that she's got a six-foot boyfriend liable to turn up any time.'

Pansy turns and darts a hostile look at us. Jessie and I attempt a smile. Still brandishing the green nail polish, Jessie says, 'I've got to show this to the girls. See you all later,' and threads her way through the throng. Harry shrugs and we move through to the dancing. It is loud and dark on the dance floor, and no one looks like they do at school. Their faces are masks of attempted cooldom now.

My stomach is knotted with nerves. I know Harry

will go off with his friends and I'll have to stay here and dance on my own. I shouldn't be here. I hate it. Dancing with Harry is disconcerting, he has a weird routine all set up and he can do moonwalking and he rotates his hips so I feel my cheeks burn with embarrassment. He flexes his hands and twists about. If I was watching him on telly I'd be really impressed, but dancing with him makes me feel really silly. Spare, in fact. He's not doing it deliberately, but his kind of dancing is showy and best done with a spotlight, not a self-conscious girl. The song never seems to end. Everyone is drinking beer or alcopops in slender glass bottles. I don't know how I will last the evening. I am thirsty and the taste of the gin lolly is still in my mouth. I want some water but am nervous of drinking anything here, in case it's spiked. Looking round the crowded room, I don't need Harry's look of surprise as I come to a grinding halt, mid-dance, to tell me I am not equipped to deal with this sort of thing. Give me a children's tea party with cupcakes any day. I must escape.

'I'm just going to the loo,' I shout. Jessie has not come back, and I want to find her.

He looks relieved and immediately heads away from the dance floor towards a gang of boys clustered around two older girls.

Outside, dusk has fallen and the street lamp on the pavement above the restaurant is throwing a fitful orange glare on the entrance. A taxi ticks up to the steps and pauses for its passenger to alight. She turns, and I am amazed to see Mum, pale yellow like Homer

Simpson in the street lighting, strain showing in the lines around her mouth.

'Lola. Oh, good! You got my message?' She comes towards me as if it is quite normal for her to have arrived at my party.

'What message? Mum, what are you doing here?' Surprise has given way to shock. No matter how much I am hating this evening, I don't need my mum to turn up. She is approaching down the steps now. I try to turn her round, shoving her a little in the small of her back. 'This is a teenagers' party. You shouldn't be here. Go away.'

But Mum stands her ground. She even grabs me by the wrist and starts hauling me up the steps.

'I'm so sorry, Lola, I had to come and get you. We must go, I need to talk to you.'

She's gone nuts. Mum has clearly lost her mind.

'No. Go away.'

I am so angry I can hardly speak. My voice has vanished to a tiny huff of fury. People from the party are looking at us in surprise. And I should think they might. Fancy coming in your office mac and suit and pearls and trying to drag your daughter away from a party she is invited to so you can talk to her.

'Leave me alone. I'm staying here,' I hiss, sounding as though I had been loving the party. 'This is the most embarrassing moment in my whole life.'

'Oh, Lola, please, come with me now.' There is sharp anguish in Mum's voice, and something in her desperate tone makes me go with her up the steps. She faces me outside the restaurant door and puts her hands on my shoulders. 'Lola, I have some sad news.

There is no easy way to tell you. Jack has died.' She pulls me towards her but I push her away, shaking my head.

'No. He can't have. You're wrong. It's his birthday next weekend and I'm going to see him.'

My voice shakes, and sobs start to thrust up through my chest. I wrap my arms across myself. Mum moves forward and this time she holds me tight. Her tears say everything.

10

Jack's funeral is on his birthday. It is the worst and the best day it could be held on. On the Norfolk train with Mum, I look out as we pass familiar landmarks. It is a cruelly beautiful day, a day meant for being outside. An estuary with the tide out, somewhere in the first hour of our journey, has the crisscross tracks of sandpipers and flat footprints of shoveller ducks in the mud. I look at it but instead I see the marshes, a low tide, and me and Jack crouched in ankle-deep water, catching flatfish in our hands. I was six the first time I caught one, and Dad has the photograph of both of us, wet and laughing, holding out our fish, Jack standing behind me in his shirtsleeves, his eyes the colour of the summer sky behind him.

'How can he not be here now?' I speak my thoughts, and am surprised to hear my voice in the quiet, early morning train carriage. Mum squeezes my hand, and I need more memories to push back the tide of loss which creeps up on me as we come nearer to Staitheley.

'Do you remember when Jack gave you Cactus?' Mum is smiling, she knows this story well too. I was

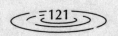

eight, carrying my book bag, back off the bus from school. Jack and Grandma had come to tea. Mum used to wear an apron a lot then and she was always baking things. I think it was jam tarts that time, but it could have been my favourite chocolate buns. She came to the door, wiping her floury hands on her blue-striped apron.

'Jack and Grandma are in the garden,' she said. 'They've got someone with them.'

I can see them still in my mind, framed by the door, in two chairs under the apple tree and Jack standing up when he saw me, leading me to the hammock, and there was Cactus asleep with a bow round his neck.

'A grown-up girl like you needs a puppy,' Jack said, and he handed me a collar and lead. 'Look after him and he will look after you.'

It was such a treat, and it wasn't even my birthday. Jack loved surprises.

In Dad's car on the way from the station, I find I am still locked in my memories. I don't want to talk. Mum and Dad are in the front. Cactus and I sit behind them and it's just like it used to be, except that everything is different. I hug Cactus, his warm round body is comforting and solid. I wish I could take him back to London with me.

'Where's Grandma?'

I can see a sliver of Dad's face in the rear-view mirror, his pale eyes like Jack's.

'At home. We're going there now to pick her up so we can all go to the church together.'

It must be the light, or just the way I'm feeling,

but Grandma's front garden with rocketing lupins and roses cascading, and the blue door in the middle of honeysuckle, is the saddest thing I have ever seen.

'I can't get out of the car, Mum,' I whisper, hugging Cactus. 'I'm afraid.'

Dad goes in, and the sight of Grandma, with her best pink lipstick on, and holding Tike in the doorway makes me feel better. I follow Mum to the house, and stand with my eyes on the floor until Grandma hugs me.

'Oh, Lola, I am so pleased to see you,' she says into my hair, and I hug her back as tightly as I possibly can. She releases me, and I struggle to make myself speak.

'I wish I had come before, Grandma, last weekend I mean.'

There. I've said it. She knows now.

Grandma squeezes my hand, and smiles.

'I know. Of course you do. And Jack knew too.'

I have never been to church without both Jack and Grandma. Often when I was small they would take me to the Sunday service and back to lunch with them afterwards, and all of us, with Mum and Dad too, attended every Easter and Christmas. We sit in the same pew as usual, but Jack is small in his coffin in front of us. Grandma is small too, and Dad and my Uncle John on either side of her are huge like rocks around her. There are too many people, all looking at me with kind, sad eyes. I know so many faces. It is bewildering to try and look at them, acknowledge them, and still keep myself from crying. I glance at Mum, she has her head down, and I copy her.

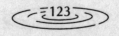

Afterwards, in the churchyard, I see Josh and his parents, and Josh nods as I pass with Grandma towards the gate. Grandma doesn't even look at Josh's mum and dad, although their faces are next to us, full of sympathy and sadness. Jack is going to be buried on Salt Head Island next to Uncle James. We have to go in boats out there. I am worried about Grandma. She is weary and cold today, and I don't think she much wants to get in a boat, but she does it, her hair ruffling in the breeze. She sits down, holding my hand tight. We are in Jack's red boat and Billy Lawson is at the helm so it is hard to believe we are not going for a picnic or fishing excursion.

'Everyone is welcome back at the village hall for tea,' shouts Dad to the people still spilling out on to the quay from the churchyard. We head out to sea with Reverend Horace and the undertakers. They are all really fisherman friends of our family, wearing hired suits and sad faces. Our family is diminished. There aren't enough with just Grandma and her two big sons, Mum and me and Great-Aunt Phyllis, Jack's sister, whom we only ever saw at Christmas when she slept through everything except the Queen's speech on telly. Phyllis has to bring her dog, a fat short-legged Labrador called Jean. Jean barks hoarsely all the time we are in the boats, but Phyllis does not utter a single word. No one does actually.

The motor chugs to life, bringing the smell of two-stroke petrol. The familiarity of the sound and scent ease my sadness as we make our way across the creek to Salt Head. The burial ground faces north, and was consecrated hundreds of years ago when there were several small houses on Salt Head. Now no one except our family is buried there – it is just too sad and lonely. The burial is surreal; I almost feel as if I am watching it from above. The things that should be very difficult, like getting the coffin off the boat, are easy, maybe because Billy and the other fishermen help Dad and John do it. Reverend Horace holds his prayer book and leads us to the burial site. The walk, which is the bit that should be easy, is so sad it is almost impossible to do. With every step I know Grandma is thinking of Uncle James as well as Jack, and I cannot stop crying. My tears are hot channels in my skin, and even the sea breeze doesn't dry them.

Mum puts her arm around me.

'Darling, Lola. I shouldn't have let you come,' she murmurs, wiping my face with her handkerchief. Her scent on it cuts through the soft, summer-marsh smell of salt water, outboard engine oil and succulent samphire. I push her away.

'No, Mum. I'm all right. I'm glad I'm here. I belong.'

I am so surprised by what I have just said that I stop crying. Mum and I look at one another in silence.

'May the Lord bless and keep the soul of our brother Jack.'

Reverend Horace used to fish with Jack for sea bass and sea trout every summer. Late at night they would head out along the Sand Bar on the Point, one in the water, waist-deep in huge waders, the other walking on the beach, a long net dragging the shallow seabed between them. In the holidays, on

Saturday nights, I was allowed to go too, and I walked behind the net with a box for the catch. Sometimes Dad came instead of Reverend Horace, and he walked deeper in the sea in his wetsuit with Jack rowing a bit further out in the darkness. The beach at night is one of my favourite places. Jack taught me to love it when I was first allowed out at night aged about seven. And I still love the glittering, mysterious night sea, and in it, just out of sight, dolphins and fish and unimaginable creatures. They are there, but we cannot see them and it is as if they inhabit a parallel world to ours as we walk on the moonlit sand.

I am wholly unprepared for the black grief which I feel when Jack's coffin is lowered into the ground and I can't see it, or remember him any more because I am crying.

My grandmother steps towards the grave and throws a tiny posy of lilac and sea lavender on the coffin. I stand by her side, calmer now, holding hands with her, until she raises her eyes to look out to sea and I know she has said goodbye.

Across the channel, a red smear catches my eye.

'They've lit the boat,' says Dad. And I can make out the dark carcass of the burning boat cloaked in flames over on the mainland. I saw them moving the boat, one of Jack's old oystercatchers, when we collected Grandma from her house, and now it is alight, and the ancient tradition feels raw and painful and matches my mood perfectly.

We chug back across the water, Grandma sitting bolt upright, her eyes never leaving the burning boat, and this time Dad guides us through the inlets to a

mooring where we can see it without being noticed too much by the crowd around it. The afternoon light melts, changes shape, and re-forms in the heat of the flames, and the black-clad mourners look like burnt scraps tossed on to the marshes by the wind as they wander back to the village hall for tea.

I walk back from the boat with Dad. We don't speak, but I hold his hand. It is cold and dry, and he walks stiffly in his dark suit and I know I cannot comfort him because when I squeeze his hand, he cannot even press my fingers in response. Mum is behind with Grandma, and when I glance back she is the only person in our group whose face is not grey. She looks separate and I don't know whether I belong with her or with Dad. I need Jack now to put everything and everyone in the right place.

We get back to the village hall and Grandma goes in, followed by a straggle of elderly ladies and her two terriers. Uncle John and Mum stand talking quietly, and Dad galvanizes himself from the spot where he has been standing, looking out across the marsh towards the island.

'I've got to go and thank people.'

He hugs me, and hurries away and it is too small a gesture from my father. I run after him. He has wet eyes and I find it hard to look at his face. I make myself smile and I put my arms around him.

'Dad, I love you so much.' I am sniffing, my face pressed against his shirt, and his warmth is reassuring.

'I love you, Lola.' He hugs my breath away and we look at each other for a moment.

*

Mum finds me playing with Sadie in the car park.

'I'm going now,' she says. 'Will you come with me?'

I nod, although the idea of anywhere existing now except here on the marshes is impossible to imagine. But being here without Jack is worse. Billy Lawson drives us to the station. As we climb up the road from the sea and over into the next valley, my phone trills, as if woken from a magic sleep. I have six messages from Harry, three from Jessie and a couple from Pansy and Freda. I have never had this many messages before. I have never had any from Harry, and now I don't want them. I read the first one. It is some rubbish about how to get a new ring tone that sounds like a loo flushing. At the end Harry has added, 'Heh Heh Atta Girl, Flash in the Pan – Yeah.' Honestly, what is the point? Does he know where I have been or what I am doing? He is an idiot. I delete everything else without reading it. The phone trills again and I look at the screen. It is from Josh at Staitheley village hall.

'*You look so sad. What can we do to help? Your loving friends Josh and Sadie Christie.*'

I turn to press my forehead against the car window so Mum doesn't see my face. I wish I had come here last weekend to see Jack. And even more I wish Mum and Dad were still together and we all lived at home in Staitheley with Cactus. It is the thought of Cactus that finally makes me howl, hugged by Mum in the back of Billy Lawson's car.

11

Back at school it is so hard to talk to anyone, and, weirdly, everyone wants to talk to me, except Freda, who doesn't like me to get too near Pansy. I couldn't care less. I hang out in the loos a lot, and if more than a day passes without me texting Nell and Josh, I get twitchy. I need the connection with home so badly, but I can't talk to Dad, it makes me too sad.

Josh is great, and we are friends now. He tells me hilarious Staitheley gossip, like this morning's snippet: 'Miss Mills isn't speaking to Mrs Wright from the shop because she heard Mrs Wright describe her dachshund as a piglet in velvet.'

I ask him about his life, but he is vague.

'Oh well, I might not do A levels. I'd like to work,' he says, his voice closed to me asking more questions. I can't imagine facing that choice, and when I talk to him, I'm glad I'm only fourteen and I am separated from those decisions by years of time. As for Harry, when I see him I feel no more than friendship and that is a relief too. I think all my emotion is used up on Jack and my family.

Mum is away again, researching for her work, and I know I have to put up with the cheesy smell of Ali's

cooking and the depressing, crunchy non-taste of bean sprouts for a couple of days at a time while Mum gets herself established. Then, she says, she'll be here much more.

Sometimes it isn't easy, though. Today when I got back, Ali had washed all her underwear and some of those awful jumpers she wears. There are pools of water everywhere and horrible grey garments in little sodden lumps on the radiators. I can normally ignore Ali's nonsense, but today it gets to me, probably because Jessie has come back with me so we can do our revision together. She is the only person at school I have told about Jack dying and she understands everything. Jessie is a real friend now, like Nell.

Jessie and I are gazing, fascinated, at the rags on the kitchen radiator when Ali walks in. She is wearing a baggy man's singlet and a lot of hair peeps from her armpit. Gross. She pushes her hair back with both hands, giving us a full-on display of her underarm hair.

'Phew, I'm baking. You create tone in your muscles if you wash your clothes yourself.'

Jessie's eyebrows are high in surprise. I grit my teeth and try to sound pleasant.

'But what's the point of having invented washing machines? It's called progress, you know,' I say without even moving my lips.

Jessie and I don't realize that we are holding our breath, waiting for a reply.

Ali speaks.

'I don't like to use machines unless essential, and for washing I think they're evil. They contain a

magnetic force that is at worst cancerous and at best energy-sapping.' She comes over to move her horrible wet clothes and Jessie and I double up in gales of silent laughter, stopping dead when she turns back to us. 'And washing your own clothes takes you back to the earth.'

'Only if you drop them when they're wet,' says Jessie, pointing behind Ali to where the porridge-coloured garments have slid off the radiator and on to the dusty floor.

We had been heating water for a Pot Noodle, but something about Ali, the hair and the clothes has completely stopped me being hungry.

'Come on, Jess, let's do some bio practice now. Then we can stop to watch the soaps before we try and tackle history.'

Jessie groans and we take our shoes off and slump on the floor in my room, the radio on full volume.

Mum doesn't actually let me watch TV until I've done all my bits of homework, and she hates me listening to the radio while I'm working, but I have to or I can't concentrate. Anyway, it's a good thing she isn't here.

Jessie twists around to make sure the door is shut and stage-whispers, 'Who is that fruitcake?'

'Mum's friend. She stays here when Mum's away.'

Jessie makes a face. 'You should watch out, you might catch something from her.'

I giggle. 'Veganism, you mean. I doubt it.' But I don't feel good talking about Ali like this. 'Mum needs someone to be here with me,' I add lamely, but

Jessie has moved on. Reaching into her bag, she pulls out a bit of paper and waves it in front of me.

'Look at this. Lascalles gave it to all of us in his tutor group, and guess who has signed up?'

'What for?' I arrange myself for maximum comfort, lying on my front on the carpet, a cushion under my chest, another under my biology folder. 'Let's do life cycles,' I suggest.

'Oh no,' moans Jessie, 'I'm so useless at everything to do with outside. Can't we do eyeballs instead?'

'Life cycles aren't necessarily outside.' I pick up the paper she has dropped next to me. 'What's this? Ohmigod, I hoped he'd forgotten about that. Surely it isn't actually going to happen?'

In Mr Lascalles's favourite font, as recognizably his as if it were handwriting, he has written:

> Pit your wits against nature and come on the Robinson Crusoe Camping weekend in Norfolk, 15–18 July. We will be living on an island, studying the flora and fauna and learning how to survive. Warden Richard Jordan of the North Norfolk Heritage Trust will instruct us on birds and tides. Are you up for a unique opportunity to go wild in the country? If so, sign below before 15 June. Open to Year 10 and above. Only 8 places available.

What a nightmare. What a bad joke it will be. How could Dad agree to it without telling me? I call him to

see if we can't cancel it, but he can't see what the problem is.

'What's wrong, Lola? We've had loads of school groups to camp on Salt Head. Why should this be different?'

'It's *my* school,' I shriek, stamping my feet all over Jessie's biology revision.

'Well, that's the best thing about it,' he says, very slowly as if talking to a Martian. 'You will be here with them.'

'I'm not coming,' I flash back instantly.

'Well, your grandmother is looking forward to it, and to meeting some of your new friends, so I hope you change your mind.' Dad's voice is so mild and melting, it makes me want to scream.

Jessie looks up when I put the phone down.

'It'll be excellent. I'm looking forward to it, and I don't usually go outside at all if I can avoid it. But this is a novelty. All the exams are over by then. It'll be a great start to the holidays. We'll get amazing tans and we can swim naked in that glittery stuff you put in your project. It'll be fab.'

She has no idea what she is talking about. I try to discourage her.

'This is Norfolk, not Fiji. It's most likely to rain, there won't be any phosphorescence and everyone will be freaked out by not having dry clothes and being covered in mud,' I mutter. 'And my dad and probably my whole family will be fussing about, keeping an eye on us.'

Of course, there is no way I can say what I really feel, which is that I can't cope with my new life and

133

my old life converging. Not even Nell, back home in Norfolk, understands. All she can do is flip through her diary in irritable frustration when I call her to tell her the bad news later that evening.

'Oh, hell. That's when I'm going on my school field trip to Wales. I won't be there except for your first night. I wonder if I could be ill and skive to see you? Look, I must go, I've got two exams back to back tomorrow, and Jason's just arrived to help me revise. Bye, darlin', catch you later.'

She presses something on her phone, but it isn't the disconnect button, and I hear her talking as she crosses the room to Jason.

'Hey, you. I'm not quite ready. Mum says do you want to stay for supper tonight?'

There is a mumble and then laughter, Nell's joined with Jason's, I suppose. I flip my phone away down the side of the bed because I don't want to hear any more of her happiness.

The trip is gathering momentum. Mr Lascalles is calling it a field trip and is issuing lists of requirements and endless forms to sign for those who want to go. There is even a consent form for sleeping in a tent, and we have to sign a declaration that girls will share with girls and boys with boys. Dad has added to the mad paper storm by sending information about nature and Salt Head for everyone to read. It is photocopied and pinned on the board next to the list of people who have put their names down.

It is too weird. Everyone wants to go on the camping trip. There's a waiting list in case anyone

drops out, and Mr Lascalles is drawing the eight names out of a hat, or so everyone says. There are rumours flying, and no one is entirely sure who has made it on to the final list. The only certainty is me, which is ironic, as I definitely don't want to go. I absolutely can't believe the popularity of the whole thing.

'Why?' I ask anyone who will listen. 'Why do you want to go and freeze your arse off in the North Sea?'

The thing is, none of them see it like that. Someone has finally learned how to spell 'Phosphorescence' and Pansy and Freda look it up on the Internet and find completely different information from the stuff I put in my project. Suddenly 'Phosphorescence' is the school buzzword.

An essay entitled 'The Phosphorescence of the Night Mushroom' appears on the general school noticeboard. It is science, but it makes no sense to any of us at all, and is the source of many jokes. Harry paints an extract of the essay in the skateboard park. 'The lamellae of the pilei are white but emit bluish white light in the dark when they are fresh.' This becomes a catch phrase around school, only eclipsed when all our e-mail accounts are hit by an attachment called 'The Palace of Phosphorescence', featuring dodgy pictures of a girl in a bikini and a chihuahua sitting on a blue towel on some beach in California. Under it is a poem about teenage suicide which, it is universally agreed, is the most moving thing anyone has ever read. Drippy Dave has the photograph printed on the front of a T-shirt, with the poem on the back, and for a week so many people follow his lead that it looks like we have embraced the notion of a uniform.

I am convinced that I am immune to any more surprises, but then Freda, who usually avoids me as if I am a toxic but highly luminous mushroom, sidles up to me at break.

'The basketball team have qualified for the National Championships, so Aiden and Tod can't go camping.'

What a relief. I have been so freaked out by the possibilities of who might be in the daunting line-up of the trip that I have actually blanked it from my mind.

Aiden and Tod wouldn't even fit on the camp beds we use on Salt Head, and imagining Dad in his Scout shorts and knee socks, them in their street-cool clothes, sends huge racking shivers of advance mortification through me.

Freda hasn't finished. She licks her thin lips delightedly, like a cat, and purrs on, her voice throbbing with innuendo and pleasure.

'So now it will be a duel over you, because your devoted wheezing admirer Dave is next on the list, along with Handsome Heart-throb Harry. It looks like this is your trip, baby.'

A challenge sparks in her slanting grey eyes. She is hoping to embarrass me, but I pretend not to notice.

'Great.' I stretch a big innocent smile and she snorts crossly, and departs, hair swinging right down her back to below her crop top.

Having thought it couldn't get worse, I then con-

template going home to Staitheley with Harry, whom I can't deny I have still got a crush on, and Dave, who can't look at me without blinking soppily. Mortifying. Maybe I could give my place up to one of Pansy's other acolytes? I doubt they'll want it now that the basketball players aren't coming. I know that Pansy is signed up, of course, but maybe she and Freda will drop out now. Oh, honestly, who gives a monkey's anyway? I might just have to eat a cyanide pill the day before – or what about a phosphorescent mushroom?

I find Jessie just as the bell goes for geography, and tell her the news. She can't stop giggling over Dave coming. I want to tell her how I dread going home to Staitheley and Jack not being there, but I can't.

I want to tell her because I don't have anyone else to talk to. Mum is back from her trip, but she is never at home. We communicate by the kitchen blackboard.

On Saturday morning I rub out her message from yesterday, which says, 'How was last exam? Eat the chicken casserole if you can face it and I'll see you for catching up tomorrow.'

I didn't eat the casserole. I had an amazingly delicious supper of potato waffles, bacon and maple syrup with *no* healthiness, to punish my absent mother. And I ate it in her bed in front of her TV and I felt truly self-sufficient and not at all self-pitying. Today, though, I could really do with seeing her. But she is obviously knackered from her work and is still asleep, even though it is ten o'clock and some of us have been up for hours and even hung up the laundry as instructed by Mum's message a few days ago.

I am writing, 'Gone BY MYSELF to Camden to buy kitchen sink etc. for camping,' when a man with rumpled hair walks out of Mum's bedroom wearing jeans, a T-shirt and bare feet. He is incredibly good-looking.

'Are you the plumber?' I ask cautiously, as for all I know this is a bloody burglar creeping about. But we have been hoping for a plumber to come for some weeks now.

'Er, no. I'm not.' He turns the tap on at the sink, and peers at the flowing water intently, as if a plumber might come out of it. 'I'm not the plumber,' he repeats, and looks desperately towards Mum's bedroom door.

I think my mouth is hanging open in astonishment, because he smiles placatingly at me, and turns off the tap, having filled the kettle.

The door to Mum's room opens again, and blow me if Mum doesn't come out wearing a pale blue silk dressing gown I've never seen before. Her hair is rumpled too, and she has a mad smirk on her face.

'I see you've met,' she simpers, and slides on to one of the tall stools we have in the kitchen.

'No. We haven't actually.' My voice is as crisp as Miss Blessup's in the school library. This is so weird and so confusing I could scream. I feel like I am the grown-up in the room, with these two looking at me nervously and edging closer to one another.

'I know you want me to make it easy for you,

Mum, but I'm not going to. Who is this man and why was he in your bedroom?'

Obviously, all the body language is screaming at me, but Mum should have told me she had a boyfriend. In fact, I should have guessed.

'Bloody hell, Mum. You could have said.' I manage to blurt these words out before the heat in my face explodes and I rush to my room and hurl myself on the bed.

I know teenagers are meant to feel misunderstood, but this is ridiculous. After a while, I realize that I'm much more upset that she hasn't told me about the boyfriend than I am that he exists.

'Lola? I'm sorry. I've mishandled this badly.' Mum is dressed. I hear the door to the flat clicking shut behind the boyfriend. I turn on my back and look at her. 'I thought he was the plumber.'

There is an uncertain silence, then we both burst out laughing.

Everyone on the trip has to meet on Monday after assembly to talk about kit, so we will see who is actually coming at last. My shopping trip with Mum was hugely successful. First we went to a cafe and drank iced coffee while she told me about meeting Marcus. I never imagined sitting chatting with my mum about boys on a Saturday morning in the High Street, but now I've done it and it was good. She didn't say anything impossible for me to hear like, 'I love him.' She just said, 'He's a kind, gentle man and being around him makes me happy.' I think I can cope with that for now. Anyway, we bought a frying

pan at the charity shop, an inflatable mattress from the camping shop and a kind of torch that looks like glasses and is usually for mechanics mending cars. She also bought me a really cool swimming costume which cost a fortune and made me look like a person with a waist, which I am not.

Marcus came back in the evening and took us out to supper. He gave me a solar-powered torch, so now I've got two, and he managed to do it without making a big deal. I think I like him. I think I like Mum with him. When added to my sleeping bag, a water carrier, a pillow, spare clothes, and a towel, my new camping stuff fills a reasonable-sized rucksack. I am a bit anxious that Mr Lascalles will make me take stuff out to make room for the food. I needn't have worried.

Our meeting is in the geography block in Mr Lascalles's classroom. It has a perfectly normal door, but in its frame Patsy and Freda are wedged like two beetles, their rucksacks and their armloads of belongings having locked together in such a way that neither of them can go out or in. The others – Jessie, Harry, Dave and two techno music heads called Carl and Pete – are inside. Not my first choice of companions but then I would rather have no one.

'It's a bit like one of those Chinese puzzles.' Harry is standing on a chair inside the classroom. He peers down at me over the girls and their rucksacks. I am suddenly so pleased that he will be coming. 'You have to find the keystone. Maybe it's Pansy's mobile phone.' Harry leans over and pulls the tiny silver phone from Pansy's pocket. Unsurprisingly, this does not help.

'Give that back!' commands Pansy between gritted teeth. 'Can't someone just take this battery charger and these CDs and then I can move.'

Leaving my rucksack against the wall, I crawl between Pansy's legs and try to extract the things she has in her right hand.

'I can't believe how much stuff you two have got,' I marvel.

'Oh, shut up, Lola,' hisses Freda, slumping suddenly as she is released by the removal of one of Pansy's many bags. But the heap around the two of them is truly extraordinary.

'Mmm, yes. I think a little judicious editing is called for.'

It is lucky Mr Lascalles didn't arrive sooner or he wouldn't have been able to get in. Now, though, he helps Pansy drag her rucksack into the room, and places his own small canvas bag on a chair.

'Right, let's write a list of essentials,' he says, stabbing one finger in the air. 'And I mean essentials.'

I rack my brains to think of anything at all that might be essential, and eventually come up with a short list:

First aid kit
Water
Food
Sleeping bag
Matches
Firewood
Spare clothes
Emergency flares

Next to me Freda is hard at work, biting the end of her pencil in concentration. Pansy's small writing flows across her page until Mr Lascalles picks up her paper with a flourish.

'Thank you, everyone. Pansy's list is the longest, so shall we all check where we coincide with her?'

Taking silence as acquiescence, he begins to read:

> *Make-up*
> *Make-up remover*
> *Mirror*
> *Shampoo*
> *Whole wash bag actually*
> *Electric toothbrush charger*
> *Nail kit including nail clippers*
> *Electric toothbrush*
> *Two skirts*
> *Three sundresses*
> *Two pairs of jeans*
> *One pair cut-off shorts*
> *Six bikinis*
> *Ski clothes for emergency weather*
> *Four towels*
> *Hairdryer . . .*

Mr Lascalles stops and screws up his face, taking off his glasses before addressing her despairingly.

'Forgive me, Pansy. Is this your list for camping?'

Pansy looks affronted.

'Yes, but I haven't even got to the tent and all the sleeping bags and stuff yet, although I have got one.'

She points to the pink and purple flowery roll tied to the bottom of her rucksack. 'Dad got it for me in Woodstock and had it sent back to be here in time. It's the best, isn't it?'

Freda is no better, although her preoccupation is keeping her clothes clean. To this end she has packed three different washing powders, a washing-up bowl and rubber gloves.

By the time the bell releases us, Mr Lascalles, looking grimly determined, and somewhat worried, has halved the size of both Pansy's and Freda's piles of belongings and removed several items from everyone else's bags.

'This is more acceptable,' he mutters, then, voicing my own thoughts, 'I wonder what the warden is going to make of you lot.' He laughs drily and gets out a map of the North Norfolk coast. 'I think it's worth looking carefully at where we are going. This may be Britain, but we are staying on an island.'

He points to Salt Head on his map. Carl and Dave look up from their rucksacks, but no one else is paying any attention.

'Hey, there's a lighthouse,' says Carl, looking at the northern end of Salt Head.

'Yes, and beyond it is Seal Point, where the currents are phenomenally dangerous.' I interrupt because I know Dad would want me to tell them this. 'We don't swim there, we go round to the beach above the burial ground.'

'How far is that from the hut?' Mr Lascalles is making notes in a small pad.

'Oh, not far. Nothing is far on Salt Head. It only

takes about twenty minutes to walk from one side to the other, but there are dunes in the middle, so you can't see everything at once. There used to be a house on it years ago, but now there's nothing left except the burial ground.'

Pansy looks up from lacing up her rucksack.

'That sounds scary,' she says with satisfaction. 'How do we escape if we want to?'

'With a boat when there is enough tide, or by waiting until it is at its lowest and wading. The currents are too strong to swim.'

I could tell them all this in my sleep, it is so familiar. Mr Lascalles slaps shut his notebook as the bell goes.

'Right, we will all have to act sensibly and carefully,' he says, staring around at the eight of us. 'I expect exemplary behaviour at all times.'

He doesn't actually click his heels together but he may as well have done.

'I'll distribute notes later in the week,' he says and walks off down the corridor, his own small bag bobbing by his side.

'He is going to be a nightmare,' predicts Harry, retrieving his mini-disc player and separate speakers and stuffing them back into his rucksack. Dave folds his pyjamas back into the side pocket of his bag, wrapping them around a bottle of what I thought was water but according to Freda's excited whisper is actually vodka.

'He won't look at the stuff again. Anyway, I'm just going to say this pocket is full of my asthma medicine.'

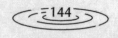

Sitting on my own bag to keep it invisible so no one notices that I have *not* been searched, I am determined not to imagine my Dad's face when we arrive in Staitheley and start trying to stash all this ridiculous stuff on the boat to get over to Salt Head Island.

Dad is so easygoing it's absurd, but not when it comes to nature conservation. Then he turns into a tinpot dictator. That was Mum's joke, anyway, and probably what made her so keen to get back to the pavements and pollution of London. In Dad's world you must treat nature with respect. No short cuts, no flip attitudes. Ideally, he would like everyone who sets foot on Salt Head to be wearing a uniform of his choosing and carrying a prescribed (by him) list of essentials. Everything else, including my Elvis T-shirt, is subject to snorts of derision and worse. I've seen him chuck whole bags full of bedding into the mud when he feels people have brought more than they need. And if he is picking the group up, and they have too many rubbish bags, he makes them carry them back on foot, wading across to Salt, the nearest village, a good hour away, because he won't take it on the boat.

'Fascist,' is actually what Mum used to say. 'Bloody fascist.' That was years ago when he tried to stop us taking streamers over there for my seventh birthday party, a beach picnic with the seals. But I know now, from that and a hundred other experiences on Salt Head Island, that everything you take must be useful and it must be working properly. I have never been over there without a life jacket and an emergency flare, but Dad is so careful I've never needed either. I don't know what he'll say about the Flower Power tent, but I can guess. I wish I hadn't seen that vodka, and I pray that Dad doesn't. I can't stop glooming out now. I know this trip is not going to work.

12

Despite my purchase of a special Romanian spell doll from the charity shop and willing the camping trip to be abandoned, the day of reckoning dawns. Mum and Marcus both take me to school, which would be embarrassing normally, but I have too much else to worry about to be concerned that I look like a juvenile delinquent being marched into care by undercover police officers.

Mum hugs me.

'Have fun, and be careful, remember these are London children. They won't have a clue about tides,' she says, pressing a tide table into my hand.

I roll my eyes.

'Honestly, Mum, are you expecting me to get them to learn this on the way up?'

But I grin and kiss her. Marcus gives me twenty quid and a BT phonecard.

'This weekend is going to be like one of those challenging TV programmes where you've got to see how far you can go with these two items,' he says, winking at me. 'I hope you will be able to get home from Staitheley.'

He kisses my cheek, which is the first time we

have touched each other, but it is not a watershed moment because I have just caught sight of Pansy's outfit for travelling and it is making me hyperventilate with anxiety about what Dad will say.

Unbelievably, we arrive in Staitheley much earlier than expected. This means that the tide is out. Pansy, chucking her phone to one side because it has had no signal for the past five minutes, leans over the seat of the minibus and shouts, 'I can see the sea. Oh. No, I can't. I can see a trickle of water and miles of mud. There isn't any sea. Where is it?'

Freda stops applying mascara to look out of the window. She wrinkles her nose.

'God, this place is filthy,' she says, and returns to the more attractive prospect of herself in the rear-view mirror.

The minibus judders to a halt. Pansy moves seats to get a better view.

'We're not stopping here, are we?' she growls, her voice at its most husky. 'We can't get out with all that mud. Where are we actually going?'

'See that hut?' I ask, pointing my finger to the tiny, Lego-sized building on the horizon, separated from us now by the thick mud of the creek at low tide. 'We're going to take a boat out there and that's where we're staying.'

'Well,' is all Pansy can say, she is so deeply shocked by the basic nature of Staitheley. She bats accusing eyelashes at me and crosses her legs, revealed to full effect beneath her white hot pants and a silver lamé halter-neck top.

'Are you auditioning for *Baywatch*?' Harry asks when she adds lipgloss and a slap of foundation before lowering her dark glasses. Pansy ignores him, and continues to gaze out of the window.

'The sun's gone,' she adds balefully.

'I think it might be your glasses,' says Jessie, not unkindly. Pansy removes them, but she was right.

In Staitheley, locals say, there is a microclimate, and we can have weather here that no one else is experiencing. It's usually quite extreme. Now the sun has rushed behind a purple cloud, and a huge shadow sweeps in across the marshes, drawing all light with it, so for a few moments the summer seems to have departed.

Along the grey quay, Dad approaches, pulling on a big yellow mac over his shorts and wellies.

'Hey, check that dude,' shouts Pete, one of the back-seat boys.

'Rock on, man. Rock right on over.'

There is a low whistle from his friend Carl.

'Clock the ear muffs.' He grins.

The last time I saw them was when Carl played an intensely cool gig for a school concert and his house won. They signed up for the trip because they thought Aiden from the basketball team was coming, and now that he's not they don't even pretend to be interested. They're just here for the ride.

My cheeks burn when I step off the coach, and, in full view of my schoolmates, am folded into Dad's arms. There is now no way I can dissociate myself from the shorts and the ear hair.

Mr Lascalles groups us around Dad on the quay and makes a little speech.

'We're all very grateful to you, Mr Jordan, for this opportunity to experience something quite unusual.'

He doesn't hear Pete whisper to Carl, 'Just how unusual is our call? D'you want a bet on Pansy?'

'Nah. Too easy. I'll go for Freda. She's more of a challenge.'

Freda bridles, obviously listening to them, not to Mr Lascalles. A huge pink ball of bubblegum swells from her mouth and she pops it with a splat over her cheek.

'Eugh, gross,' she squeals, cutting through Mr Lascalles's thanks.

Dad coughs, delivers a flinty glare at our assembled group and begins his spiel.

'Right, you lot. I'd like you to listen carefully for a few moments and then I'd like you to go away and digest what I am about to tell you. This is not chit-chat. Your lives might depend on your listening to me.'

I have heard it loads of times before, so I really can't be expected to listen. But he has caught the others' attention, at least for the time being. I glance around surreptitiously, horribly aware of the spectacle we are creating on the quay.

Caroline Christie drives past, and I see her raise her eyebrows as Pansy, clearly wanting to change the tempo, reaches her arms above her head in a stretch which reveals yet more of her perfect midriff. Dad has lost everyone's attention already, and he has only got to the bit about not disturbing the terns. I switch off for a while, coming to with a start when he puts his arm around me again (why is he doing all this friendly stuff? It's not normal) and says, 'Anyway, I know I can trust my daughter to show you all how to behave on the nature reserve. Look to Lola's example and you won't go far wrong.'

How could he? What have I done, apart from not listening, to deserve this sort of humiliation? Crimson, I mutter something inarticulate and step casually out of his embrace. All the time we have been talking, the tide has been creeping up. We hang around waiting for it to be high enough to set off.

An old rowing boat with an outboard engine slides alongside us and I cannot believe the way things can go on getting worse. It is Josh and his dad, and they are taking us out to Salt Head. It could have been any one of the fishermen around here, but no, it has to be Josh. Why didn't he tell me he was taking us? I am not prepared for mixing my two lives. Panicking, I scramble to the opposite end of the boat from where I know he will be sitting.

'I am due at an emergency meeting this afternoon, so I can't come over with you,' Dad is explaining to Mr Lascalles. 'The only people I could get were Ian Christie and his son, Josh. So they will take care of you all.'

'Blimey, don't spare us, will you?' mutters Josh's dad under his breath, winking a greeting to me.

I can hardly look at him. I still don't understand why Dad can't relax with them. I want to talk to Josh about it right now, to clear it up once and for all, so we can all accept that James died and Ian lived and

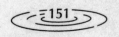

that it's sad but it was all so long ago. I feel like the grown-up with Dad right now, even in the middle of my embarrassment. Annoyingly, Josh makes sure he doesn't catch my eye as he heaves all our belongings into a dinghy attached to the motorboat. Dad, having looked Pansy up and down very slowly, has not attempted to edit our luggage at all, and soon the boat is sinking close to its Plimsoll line.

'All right, get in. Girls at the front, please.'

Freda, pausing to apply some fudge-scented hair mascara in vivid pink, joins me at the front.

'He's fit.' She glances at Josh, who's helping Pansy into the boat. 'Do you know him?'

'Of course I do, I know everyone in this village. There are more people in our school than live here, you know.'

Freda is surprised I am so short with her,

'All right, keep your hair on. Oh look, Pansy's playing her tricks on him.'

At the other end of the boat, Pansy is perching next to the outboard, tying a shawl over her hair and shooting sideways glances at Josh as he unties the mooring line, making sure the small dinghy he is pulling behind doesn't get caught in any ropes.

'How did she manage to get to sit next to him?' hisses Freda.

'She won't be able to when we set off.'

And indeed, Josh places a hand under Pansy's elbow and propels her to the bench in front of us.

'God, he's right up my street, girls,' Pansy announces gladly and, getting out her phone, waves it in the air in search of a signal. 'I've got to tell everyone about this guy. He's so gorgeous. What's his name, Lola? How old?'

The engine has started, but even so, Pansy's voice is easily heard. She sounds as if she is talking about a pet guinea pig. Josh sets his jaw and looks out to sea. His dad shoots Pansy a look of disgust that makes my toes curl. She, however, is oblivious.

'God, how do they survive out here? No signal at all,' she shrieks. 'I'll have to put a message in a bottle, or maybe I'll just keep him all to myself and not tell anyone how lovely he is. What did you say his name was, Lola?'

I want to catch Josh's eye, so I can wordlessly tell him I am not part of this, but he will not look at any of us.

Next to Pansy, Jessie suddenly swoops towards the water. Leaning forward to grab her, I find she is giggling.

'Did you think I was going in? Don't worry, I just had to test the water. Its freezing, isn't it? I hope everyone has got wetsuits. I know I have.'

'Well, we don't heat it for tourists,' says Josh coldly.

Up in the front, Harry is delving in his rucksack for gloves and a hat. Pete and Carl have got their headphones on. The only person treating Josh and his dad normally is weedy Dave, whom I can see mouthing some sort of conversation with them.

The tide is 'out' and 'low'. How can it come in so fast, with enough water to set off in the boat? We bounce over the waves to Salt Head, and with every breath the familiar exhilaration of being on the sea

comes back to me. The sun is over the dunes at the tip of the island now and, squinting to look at the familiar landscape, I am suddenly flooded with sadness for Jack. I wish my family was whole again.

The tide has turned when we finally reach the island, and we cannot get the boats right up.

'Everyone out,' says Ian, cutting the motor.

'But we're not at the edge,' objects Pansy. 'We'll get soaked.'

Mr Lascalles has taken off his shoes. He rolls up his shorts so they are embarrassingly brief, and jumps in up to his thighs.

'Welcome to the world of camping. We can't get right to the land because the boats can't go any shallower or they will be grounded,' he says to Pansy, and holds a hand out to help her from the boat.

'This is so not glamorous,' she sighs, but drops into the water with no more complaints.

When we are all standing in the water, Josh passes Mr Lascalles the rope of the smaller boat.

'You can drag this one up on that mud to get your stuff on dry land, but then you'll need to wade out a bit further than here to anchor it. It gives you more leeway with coming and going.'

'And be quick with it or you'll end up stranded with it on the mudbank,' shouts his dad. Standing by the tiller, Josh salutes us mockingly as they depart.

Even Mr Lascalles has a slightly forlorn note to his voice as he begins to take charge.

'OK, Carl and Pete, could you take the first bags over? Harry, anchor the boat here, will you? I don't

see a need to drag it through the mud. We can wade with the equipment.'

'You must be mad,' mutters Freda, floundering through thick oozing mud to the shore with her rucksack. 'Urgh, this mud smells disgusting.'

'Oh, stop moaning.' Pete chucks a tent down next to her. 'Here, carry this stuff up to the hut.'

Astonishingly, Pansy has made no fuss at all, but wordlessly shoulders her vast floral rucksack and wades to the edge with it.

'I'm going up to the campsite,' she volunteers. 'I'll start unpacking.'

The campsite is dominated by the lookout hut, a small, breezeblock house with a tiled roof, a fireplace and no loo, water or electricity. Really it is little more than a lean-to with damp, peeling brick walls. I love it. I have stayed in it every summer and sometimes at other times of the year too. It has bunk beds and a tiny loft reached by a ladder where you have a view over the sandbank and out to sea. The other windows face Staitheley. It is much more primitive than Pansy's tent, but, with a kitchen table, crockery and even a pack of slightly frilly, damp cards, it is a base I know we will be glad of.

Mr Lascalles is breathless and caked in black mud when he finally sets foot in the hut. He doesn't seem unduly bothered by the mushrooming chaos of Pansy's unpacking.

'I'm ready for a swim before we get this place sorted for the night. Lola, take us to the best beach around if you please.'

Suddenly, I am giddy with anticipation. We are

here. None of them really knows what to expect, and it isn't raining.

I am the last into the sea, because I want to see everyone else go in. I feel like I used to when I was little at my birthday parties. I would sometimes just stop and stand still, smiling and looking around at everybody enjoying themselves. Mr Lascalles is so white he looks as if he is wearing a T-shirt, but he dives beneath a wave and strikes out along the shore, swimming strongly. Harry has brought a boogie board, and he and Carl muck about, trying to stand up on it. Pete wolf-whistles as Pansy edges towards the water in a searingly bright yellow bikini. Taking a puff of an inhaler, Dave runs up behind her but is pushed in by Freda and Jessie, both wearing goggles and wetsuits, which on a summer afternoon is absurd, but entertaining to look at.

The swim is an icebreaker. Afterwards, Mr Lascalles goes for a walk up to the end of the island at Seal Point and I take some of the others over to the creek side facing Hinkley Marshes to catch flatfish in the warm shallow water.

'You stand still and watch the water. When you see the sand move, you have to shove your hands in fast and if you're quick you will catch a flatfish and we can cook it.'

Harry and Pansy, Pete, Freda and Carl look at me in amazement.

'That is wild.' Carl begins to roll up his jeans.

'You're saying you can catch them in your hands?' Harry wrinkles his nose in disbelief.

'It is so *Robinson Crusoe*,' marvels Pansy. 'I love

that lighthouse.' And she squints into the sun, pointing at the old striped tower up by Seal Point.

'Hey, look!' Pete is already in the ankle-deep water, poised. 'I see it. I always thought that scuttling of something along the seabed was a crab.'

I have to say I really enjoy this moment of power. All of them are so impressed by something so simple. I am the epitome of confident success. Yippee. I wade into the water to demonstrate and, shrieking, dive in pursuit of a scuttling stream of sand. Of course, I lose my balance and fall flat on my face in the shallows.

'Missed it!' I yell, laughing, partly because they look so amazed, so clean and so timid.

'I think I'll watch,' says Harry, tossing the little dice he keeps in his pocket. 'I'll have a quiet bet with myself over who will catch the most.'

I raise my eyebrows at him. I am aware of a stab of disappointment, because he is only watching, because he doesn't want to risk looking foolish.

We cook sausages on the little hearth outside the hut. Pansy makes a washing line with a length of ribbon she has brought, and hangs our wet clothes above the fire. Harry is the least helpful person once again, and sits on an upturned bucket, teasing Jessie about the pile of bird and plant books she has brought.

'Looks like you'll be up all night reading these,' he says, flipping through a pocket wild-flower guide, before chucking it on the ground. Pansy turns on him.

'Harry, why don't you do something useful, like gather some wood?' she suggests.

He stands to attention, mocking her.

'Yes, ma'am. Where from, ma'am?'

I roll my eyes and stretch my arm to encompass the whole island.

'Use your common sense,' I hiss, still irritated by him.

He wanders off, and when he reappears by the fire, he has a crate of neatly stacked wood with him and a spray of rugosa roses.

'This might be nice as a centrepiece for the table,' he suggests, giving it to me.

'Did you find that?' I am curious. I know there is a wild rose bush on the Point, but it is way up on the other side, by James's and Jack's graves. I don't think he could have found it in the time he has been gone.

He shakes his head.

'No, someone gave it to me.'

'Who?' I demand.

Harry smiles and jerks his head back.

'A mermaid. She's just getting dressed. We had a swim.'

It is irrational, I know, but I am really irritated by the news that he has just gone off on his own for a swim. Or even with someone. I am about to interrogate him on who the mermaid is when Pansy shrieks with joy. She has climbed on to the roof of the hut and has found a signal.

'Guys, it works, it works! Does anyone want me to get a message to anyone?'

'You should get off there. The coastguards have binoculars trained on this place, and if they see you up there you'll be kicked out.'

The voice of reason coming round the corner is Nell.

'I didn't know you were coming!'

I rush to hug her.

'I didn't either, but my mum was in Salt and I suddenly decided to walk up and see you, so here I am until the next tide takes me out of here.'

'Or until you walk back.'

I am amazed that these unwelcoming words are coming from me, but instinctively I am bristling with antagonism. I don't want Nell here. This is my thing with my new school. She does not belong. Harry comes over with the rose in a jam jar.

'Welcome to our island retreat,' he says mockingly, and it doesn't take Einstein to figure out that he fancies Nell.

'Hey, Lola, there's a call for you.' Pansy has got all our phones balanced on the chimney of the hut and is playing at being receptionist. 'It's that hunky guy, Josh. Shall I take a message for you?'

She giggles flirtatiously into the phone. Hastily I scramble up on to the roof and take the phone gingerly, not wanting to lose the signal.

'You're an idiot to let your friends get on the roof, Lola,' is how Josh greets me.

'You shouldn't be spying,' I respond, hurt, and feeling persecuted on all sides.

'I'm not. Your dad asked me to keep an eye on you with the telescope.'

Oh, that's great, isn't it? Dad asks Josh to look out for us. Josh, of all people. He doesn't even like him.

'Well, there's no need for you to go on watching us. We're fine.'

From up here I have a bird's-eye view of Carl, natty in his yellow billowing shorts, dragging one of the canoes that are kept by the hut right through the oystercatchers' nesting area towards the sea. I pray Josh doesn't see that.

'Um, I'd better go,' I mutter. But not quick enough.

'Tell that idiot with the really sad shorts to get away from the birds, Lola.' Josh pauses, then adds, 'Oh, and be careful of fires. There could be one starting behind you right now.'

I swivel in time to see Pete approaching with a lit cigarette. God, they are all so lawless. I wish Mr Lascalles had brought a sidekick to keep control when he wanders off to commune with nature.

'Oh, leave us alone,' I snap at Josh. 'God, we're supposed to be on holiday, not in a sodding military camp.'

I hurl my phone off the roof and it thuds on the ground next to Freda. The sausages are done. Harry builds up the fire and we sit round it, waiting for Mr Lascalles, thawing out privacy and self-consciousness. I remain silent and inhibited until Nell, with a sigh, stands up and announces that she must go.

'I thought you were waiting for the next tide.' Harry jumps up too.

'I can't, I've got stuff to do. I'll swim if I have to.'

Her hair is piled in a high knot, with curls escaping. She is thinner than when I last saw her, and she moves with a luxurious confidence that is

mesmerizing. Or so Harry seems to think. A flame of loathing for my best friend shoots through me. She's showing off – she knows it's too dangerous to swim.

'Bye, Nell,' I shout, busying myself with the washing-up Jessie is piling in the biggest saucepan. 'Thanks for coming.'

Nell looks anxious for a minute, then turns away.

'I'll see you soon,' she calls.

'I'll walk you part of the way,' offers Harry.

My choked fury is interrupted by Pansy, still on her own mission.

'Is there a mirror anywhere? I desperately need to pluck my eyebrows,' she says, brandishing a torch.

Jessie and I subside, giggling, on the sleeping bags we have hurled in a heap by the fire, ready to sort for sleeping out on later. It is dark now, and Mr Lascalles finally comes to from his reverie to take charge. He has been reading the comment book from the hut, and now he slaps it shut.

'No mirrors. But could everyone make their beds up now and start thinking about putting the camp to bed,' he says, and is interrupted by weedy Dave, whom I suspect has been knocking back the vodka.

'Mr Lascalles, it's only ten o'clock. What about a dune expedition now? We could reconnoitre for the morning mission.'

'You may do as you please as long as you are careful,' says Mr Lascalles, who has become so relaxed and benign it is creepy. 'I am going to turn in now.' He continues, 'I want to be up at dawn to observe the birdlife here. I cannot bear to miss a moment of

daylight. I'd like you all to stay within hearing of the camp.'

Then he makes his big mistake. He drops his box of earplugs and we all watch the little wax balls spill on the ground, rolling out into the beam of his torch as he bends to pick it up. If I wasn't so cross about Nell and Josh spying, I'd be thrilled. The teacher, who seems to have abdicated any responsibility because he is so entranced by nature, is putting earplugs in and going to bed. There is a full moon, the night is young, and we are eight teenagers alone on an island.

13

'Hand in hand, on the edge of the sand,
  they danced by the light of the moon,
    the moon,
  they danced by the light of the moon.'

'Come on, let's go skinny-dipping,' squeaks Jessie, who, along with Dave, has been drinking vodka with a straw out of his rucksack pocket and giggling over the washing up. They skip ahead towards the sea singing 'The Owl and the Pussy-Cat' and in a moment are invisible, swallowed by the inky late evening light, although their voices are still audible. Mr Lascalles is in his tent, the light from his tilley lamp creating a warm red glow so the tent is a tiny echo of the sunset before the last glimpse sinks beneath the horizon.

I don't feel guilty about Mr Lascalles, because I reckon the sea is within hearing of the camp, and I don't really feel I am disobeying Dad's constantly repeated rule that an adult should be aware when you swim off Salt Head, because Harry is seventeen and that is more or less an adult, in some areas of life any-way.

'Let's go up to the dunes and have a game to warm up, and then find those two and swim.'

Harry lopes past me, barefoot and chucking a Frisbee straight up in the air, spinning it so it comes back down to him. Pete and Carl are on the shore, walking with Pansy up the beach in the direction Harry has indicated.

'This is amazing.' Freda catches me up. She is muddy and crumpled and her hair is all over her face. Her eyes are shining. 'I can't believe this place can be real. I've just found a nest in the stones, just a little hollow with two pale grey eggs in it. It's like a magic sign or something. Thank you so much for bringing us here, Lola,'

I am so grateful for her enthusiasm I could cry. We link arms and crunch along the shingle. The sun has set over the horizon, but pink still floods on to the surface of the sea, casting a faint glow on to us as we walk along the beach.

'If this place was somewhere hot, it would be mega crowded,' Freda adds.

'But it was quite hot today,' I point out. 'And – oh no, what has he got?'

This is under my breath as Harry sprints towards us with a coil of netting in his hands.

'Look what I found,' he shouts. 'We can use this as a football goal.'

'You can't,' I reply, struggling to keep my voice steady. 'That's my grandfather's sea bass net, or if it's not his, it'll be someone else's.'

I feel violated, almost as if someone had walked into my house and taken all my most precious things.

I know I am overreacting, but I can't help it because it is Jack's.

'But it was just lying on the beach over there,' protests Harry, pointing to where I can just see the hump of an upturned boat. Jack's boat. The one he used to take out for the sea bass. Tonight would be a perfect night for it. Tears blur my eyes, and I press my fingers into them. Harry is really winding me up by arguing, and I think he's doing it on purpose. He must be, no one could be so insensitive by mistake.

'You can't take things just because they're lying around. People leave things here because it's safe.'

I grab the net from his hands, and it falls, tangling and snagging, on to the shingle.

'All right, keep your hair on.' Harry makes a face at me, and Freda, behind me, giggles.

There is a shout from Carl, climbing a dune behind Pansy and Pete.

'Hey, Lola, come and tell us about the tower.' He points to the lighthouse, a grey column just discernible in the darkness as the moon sails out from behind a bank of low cloud.

'It's the lighthouse. It isn't used any more. They used to use gas lamps in it, when my grandad was young, and he told me that they brought the gas for it by pony and cart from Salt. There used to be a way over the marsh in those days.'

'Why didn't they just put it in a boat?' Carl has waited for us, but the others have disappeared, and I suddenly realize that weedy Dave and Jessie have been gone for ages.

'Oh, the currents are too unpredictable and the

undertow is terrible.' I run up the next dune, anxious to find everyone. 'That's why there's a lighthouse here. Seal Point is like an island that gets exposed at low tide but when the tide is high you don't know it's there underneath the water and boats can get stuck on it.'

Carl is behind me.

'Do wrecks still happen? I thought they went out with the pirates and pantomime years ago.'

I can't see Dave and Jessie anywhere, and I feel worried and distracted.

'Oh, yes. Boats get grounded quite often, but not right here because the coastline has changed and the channel around Salt Head is deeper than it used to be. The sea changes things all the time.'

I am running now, and calling out, 'Where are you?'

Darkness is creeping off the sea, and although I can make out the humps and hillocks of the landscape, I can't see any of the others.

Harry, Freda, Carl and I stand for a moment on the highest dune, looking in all directions. Back towards Salt we can see the tiny ember-red glow of Mr Lascalles's tent, but it is a long way back, and I know that this is the only point it can be seen from in the dunes.

'They won't know where they are.' Freda's voice is strained and nervous.

'And the dunes are huge. They must stretch for twenty minutes in each direction,' says Carl.

'We could shout,' I suggest. 'But the sound carries

weirdly here, and Mr Lascalles will probably hear if we do.'

'I think we should light a fire here and it will attract them. They'll definitely see it on top of this dune.'

Harry's suggestion for once seems sensible. He and Carl run down towards the sea to look for driftwood.

'Sh, listen,' I whisper to Freda. 'We'll hear them talking.' But the rush and slap of waves hitting the beach are the only sounds around us.

I know Freda is scared, because she is stiff with silence and standing as close to me as is possible without actually hugging me.

'What if someone else finds us before the others come back?'

I put my arm around her.

'It's all right, Freda, there isn't anyone on the island at night.'

'But there are spooks and spectres,' hisses a rasping voice behind us.

Freda screams, and so do I, feeling foolish and clamping my hand over my mouth immediately.

It is Pansy, who has sneaked up the dune to us with Pete.

'We've been for a swim,' she announces. 'It's lovely.'

I would gaze at her astonished if I could see her in the dark, but I can't, so can only marvel to myself at the hearty outdoorness of Pansy. I never would have thought it of her. Harry and Carl call from the bottom of the sand dune.

'We're doing the fire here on the beach so we can come back to it when we've swum.'

An orange flame flickers below us, and we run down, feet sinking in the cool, giving sand. The fire takes fast, and stretching my hands in front of it I notice a twist of rope, a broken board with most of a notice saying:

ICE REAMS
50P OR 90P
ITH FLAKES

It is the ice-cream sign on Dad's warden's hut, which opens as a tiny cafe in the summer when school parties come over. They must have ripped it off the wall. The fire sinks a little and a pole rolls into the cinders. Jack's pole that he used in his little boat to hook up the net with.

'Where did you get this stuff to burn?' My tone is so casual that no one pays any attention, so I sidle up to Carl and ask again, 'Where did you find the stuff for the fire?'

'Oh, it was by that boat. I think it's some of the fisherman's stuff, but I don't reckon we'll be caught.'

'No, it's fine.' Harry chucks what looks to me like an oar on to the fire. 'It's a great blaze, isn't it?'

This is a nightmare. I don't know what to do. I don't know how to stop them destroying what needs protecting here on Salt Head. I turn away from the fire, and move into the darkness beyond its glow and begin to walk to the sea.

'I'm going for a swim,' I call, when I hope I am far enough away for no one to follow me.

I am so angry that I don't even think twice about taking every item of clothing off and walking straight into the sea. I am soon up to my waist. Automatically I suck in my stomach, something I have done whenever I swim since I was little and worked out that holding my breath meant less circumference of tummy would be in the water. Something like that. Anyway, whatever. It's a habit. And I am in properly now, silky water over my shoulders, bubbles rushing as I duck-dive to wet my head. My brain cools, and I know it isn't Harry and the others I'm angry with. It's myself for being too keen to impress them. It was up to me to stop them burning equipment, and I said nothing because I wanted everyone to like me. I didn't want to be the killjoy, but they won't know any better unless I tell them. I kick my legs and a spray of light green bubbles bursts in my wake. Raising an arm, I turn in the moonlight, drops cascading around me.

'Cool. This is wicked, man.' Harry is in the water with me, and behind him I can hear the others shrieking and giggling on the edge. I don't want to be left with just Harry.

'Come on in,' I shout, treading water. 'The phosphorescence is fantastic tonight.'

'Where are you?' Freda is the nearest, but then she shrieks, 'Oh no! There was something gliding past. It's a monster.'

Screaming, half with laughter and half in fright, she runs out.

'Of course there isn't,' I shout, and Harry, next to me, says, 'You are a cool babe, Lola. Is there anything you're scared of?'

It is amazing what a compliment can do to soothe a ruffled temper. The others in the shallows splash after Freda, and I can see them running in and out of the water, laughing and daring one another to go further in again. I don't think they'll come as far out as we are. I lie on my back and flick my legs lazily. Harry dives down, a trail of pale green fire following him, and emerges on the other side of me, a luminous spray arcing behind him when he tosses his head back.

'Come on, let's go on,' he says, leading me deeper into the glittering sea. And suddenly my heart is pounding with excitement, and my irritation with him has vanished. I am naked in the sea with a boy. The sea is cool and taut when I stretch my legs and kick or dive, pressing onwards beneath the surface. I am out of my depth. I laugh out loud, because of the pun. I half wish the others would catch up, and half pray that they don't. My head is the only bit of me that feels cold, but when I dive, I am warm all over.

'Can they see us?'

Harry is right in front of me, luminous skin, eyes shaded by the fall of the moonlight. He puts one hand under my chin and kisses my mouth, treading water. All I can think as I kiss him back is that I am not sure if this counts as a snog. We sink together and green sequins flash and sparkle around us. It is exactly like being in a Walt Disney movie. It is brilliant.

*

The others are sitting by the fire when we come out of the water. I had forgotten about getting out if you are naked, but Harry behaves as if it is perfectly normal, so, looking anywhere except at him, I try and do the same.

'Pulling on jeans over wet legs on sand could be a good race, like the sack race,' I gasp.

Harry is already dressed, and looking towards the fire.

'You know what?' he says. 'Dave and Jessie aren't here, and they should have seen the fire and found their way back by now.'

'They'll be all right.' I don't know what I'm talking about, but I don't want to wake up from this magic spell of having swum with Harry. He is so nice to be with, rubbing my back when I shiver, and smiling secret messages to me. Honestly, I could melt. I don't know how I was annoyed with him, but it has vanished now.

At the fire, Carl and Pete are smoking cigarettes, holding them between thumb and forefinger.

'Any sign of the others?' Harry asks.

Crouched by the fire, absorbing its heat, there is no excuse for me to say, 'Don't worry, I know they're fine. They'll be back at camp.' Of course, I don't know anything of the sort. In fact, I know enough about being out here to send everyone home screaming with their hair standing on end if I chose to tell the wedding dress story, or any other legend about the Point. But I don't. Carl throws his cigarette end into the fire, and I try and look nonchalant like everyone else.

'I think we should go and look for them,' says Carl. 'Then we'll be able to chill out and listen to a bit of music.'

I wonder if he has remembered to charge his iPod, but I say nothing. All I am interested in is preserving this mood with Harry. This involves standing right against him, brushing my hands past his, and then, when we have kicked sand into the fire, walking so close I can feel the heat of his body down my side.

Everyone is acting as though me and Harry being together is normal. I love it. It makes me smile in the dark as we walk back down the shore towards our camp. As we approach, I begin to pray that they are there, and I hold on to Harry and follow close behind Freda and Pansy, willing Dave and Jessie to appear.

The camp is silent and still, the fire has burnt down to embers which give off the only light. Further off, Mr Lascalles's tent is in darkness, but the door of the lookout hut is ajar. Pansy pushes it open.

'Here you are,' she cries.

'Sh,' whispers everyone else, crowding behind l er into the little room.

Inside, a candle gutters on the table, a fire smoulders in the grate and yet more wet clothes are hanging off the mantelpiece. The smiling and somewhat glazed faces of Jessie and Dave loom from the darkness. Next to the candle is Dave's bottle of vodka and a pack of cards.

'We're having a game of cards,' says Dave, speaking very slowly and trying to decide where to fix his

gaze. Jessie is wrapped in a towel, but doesn't seem to be wearing much else. She hiccups and giggles.

'I've lost everything, my underwear, my innocence, my—'

'All right, all right, steady.' Carl pats her on the back. 'That's enough now.'

'They're drunk.' I am surprised to hear the shock in Pansy's voice. I thought she was the type to have been drinking people under the table since she was about seven. 'What shall we do?'

Pete takes the bottle, now only a quarter full, off the table and puts it on a shelf.

'We should all go to bed. If we get caught with you two in this state there's going to be hell to pay.'

It is hard not to aim a kick at the sniggering, lolling pair as we guide them out of the hut and across to their tents. They make no attempt to keep quiet, and the rest of us are whispering and tiptoeing in anxiety. If Mr Lascalles wakes up, they'll probably be expelled for this. Shunting Jessie through the door of Pansy's tent, I have to remind myself to be kind, in order that I don't just leave her. Pansy and I heave her legs into the sleeping bag, leave her wrapped in her towel inside it and creep out again.

'Could I squeeze in with you and Freda?' Pansy whispers to me. 'I bet she'll snore. Drunk people always do.'

'I think I might sleep outside,' I say, tentatively but loud enough for the boys to hear. 'That was the idea earlier. We've just got to make the beds up.'

I am still keen to keep some sort of spell going

and, also, I am pretty sure none of the others has ever slept outside, and they will love it.

'Can you sleep outside?'

'What if it rains?'

'Isn't it freezing?'

Everyone crowds around me, and Harry grins and says, 'Come on then, Lola. Lead the way and we'll do it. But what do we sleep on?'

14

A piping birdcall close to my ear wakes me, and beyond it I hear the clamour of gulls and the sea whispering. A breeze plays around my head, and I put up my hand and find my nose is frozen, but the rest of me, inside my sleeping bag, is warm and heavy. Opening my eyes, a dazzle of light, pale gold and blue, hits me and I blink several times before I can see properly. Leaning up on my elbows I survey the camp and wish so much that I had a camera.

The fire still smoulders and around it, like moored barges, our camp beds are positioned end to end. On each bed, a mound of sleeping bags and coats lies inert and slug-like, only the different mops of hair poking out at the end suggest the identities of the sleepers. With difficulty, I wriggle out of my cosy hollow and build the fire up again. I don't know what time it is, but it must be early because Mr Lascalles hasn't unzipped his tent yet, despite his plans for dawn birdwatching.

I am the only person awake and the kingdom of the island belongs to me. It won't last though. The fire is blazing again, and soon everyone will get up and begin cooking bacon and boiling the kettle. I

realize that this is the moment to slip away to Jack's grave. I couldn't bear anyone here to even ask where I'm going. Jack doesn't belong to my new life, he is the centre of my old one, and I need to say goodbye to him alone.

The grave looks different now. It is no longer a raw new scar, but part of Salt Head. Vetch and sea holly have scrambled over it, and Dad has put up a simple wooden cross. The inscription reads, 'In loving memory of Jack Jordan, who lived on and loved the sea.' With the dates of his birth and death.

The breeze had been getting stronger, but at Jack's grave the air is still. I look up at the pale blue sky and see the dot of a lark, its voice tumbling towards the earth. I have the weirdest raw-egg sensation. I feel that I have a shell and I am only aware of having it because it has just cracked in two and sadness is welling out everywhere. The morning is clear overhead, although, on the horizon, the purple bruise of a storm is coming. It is an effort to leave. I can feel my grandfather's presence so strongly here. James's grave is less shocking now it has been joined by Jack's, and the tearing grief of the place has gone. It has become peaceful. I wonder if Grandma ever comes across here.

Freda and Carl are squatting by the fire, prodding bacon in a smoke-blackened pan. It has taken no time for them to adopt primitive habits, and all of us are beginning to look mad.

'I don't suppose anyone has a mirror?' Pansy has not yet given up on her appearance. 'Mr Lascalles confiscated mine back at school.'

'The nearest we can muster is a piece of silver foil,' offers Mr Lascalles, smoothing a scrap he has just unwrapped from the sausages.

'Oh, thanks,' says Pansy, rolling her eyes and sighing. 'I may as well go and find a puddle to look in.'

I try to deflect her.

'I don't think it's a good idea to know what you look like when you're out here. You can imagine from the state of the others, but even if you did see, there would be nothing you could do. It's not like hair straighteners are available.'

Pansy stares at Freda, with her bird's-nest hair and soot on her nose, and then at me. I can only imagine that I look filthy and slaggish, as Pansy shakes her head.

'No,' she says, 'I don't think I can possibly imagine myself from the state of you lot. And anyway, I don't want to imagine.' She presses her hands against her cheeks, and I can't tell if she is in mock distress or real. 'But I have to see myself in the mirror. It's something I've done every day of my life. I thought Jessie might have one, but she's just groaning in my tent and won't come out. She says she needs to talk to you, by the way.'

Realizing it is useless to reason with her, I abandon Pansy and crawl into the purple tent. Inside, mauve light figured with daisies casts an unhealthy shadow across Jessie's face.

The tent smells of stale alcohol, and poor Jessie has tears sliding on to her pillow.

'I think I've got tonsillitis,' she croaks. I put my

hand on her forehead. It is hot and dry. She flinches. 'Everyone will think it's a hangover,' she weeps, 'and I've probably got that too, but my throat is agony. Is there a doctor near here?'

Nodding, I crawl back out to get Mr Lascalles.

'Lucky the tide is right or we'd have to walk with her,' he says, putting away the bird book and the SAS handbook which he has been studying. 'What a pity. I was going to do something on scavenging food and also sea safety. It will have to wait though.'

Mr Lascalles sets off, pulling the dinghy on its long mooring rope as close to the beach as he can, and helping poor Jessie climb into it. She sits miserably beside him, looking as though she has swallowed two golf balls and they have lodged in her neck. Pansy goes with them.

'I just think I need to see a pavement,' she says. 'I know it's only a village pavement, but it's better than nothing.'

'Yeah, and they've got mirrors in the Staitheley Hotel loos,' adds Harry cynically as we wave them off. Carl and Pete are also in the boat, Mr Lascalles having decided that he needs some manpower in case of emergency.

'And as for the rest of you, please just take it easy around the camp till I'm back,' he shouts across the water.

The little dinghy is filled to capacity with five people in it. The swell rocks it as Mr Lascalles and Pete heave on the oars, fighting the pull of the outgoing tide. Carl holds the tiller ready to start the engine as soon as they reach deeper water.

'And then there were four. Except Dave hasn't surfaced yet,' says Harry, turning away and taking a running jump towards Dave's tent.

'Come on, man. Get up! We need to go on a mission, while the tide is still here at all,' he yells, levering himself in through the opening.

Freda follows, kneeling outside and shouting, 'Yes, come on. We want to go and swim with the seals. Mr Lascalles told us where they are at breakfast. We've got the map. We're going in the canoes.'

'I think we should stick around here.'

I am embarrassed to be the voice of reason, as usual, and none of them hear me except Freda.

The tent is rocking as Harry and Dave tussle over Dave's removal from his sleeping bag.

Freda throws me a scornful look.

'No way, Lola. You can come out here and do this stuff all the time, but for us this is really exciting.'

Freda is assertive and excited, quite different from her cool school persona. She doesn't need to be Pansy's sidekick any more. She is here in her own right and she loves it. Her eyes glitter as she pulls on her jeans and ties her matted hair in a ponytail.

'Come on, we'll see so much. We need to get going, the tide is going out.'

In my head, as persistent as the sea, is my dad's voice telling me never to set out from Salt Head on an outgoing tide; the current can sweep you away if you haven't got a reliable engine.

'I think it would be better to wait until the tide comes in again. It could be dangerous.'

But suddenly they are all experts on the sea.

'Oh no! Don't be pathetic. We want to go over to Seal Point and Mr Lascalles and your dad both told us you can only see it properly at low tide.'

'Yes, but you can't land on it.' I am impatient. 'It is forbidden to actually set foot on it.' I now see what Dad means when he says that no one listens. 'It isn't safe on Seal Point. There's quicksand for one thing, and the tide races in and you can get caught in some powerful currents.'

'Excellent,' mumbles Dave, doing up his belt as he joins us, a bacon sandwich wedged in his mouth. 'We'll have to be incredibly precise. It's so cool, it's a life and death thing.'

I sometimes get nightmares where I am trying to speak but no sound comes out of my mouth. In those dreams I try to move, maybe just to write down what I can't say, but my limbs are so heavy and I am so sinkingly tired that there is nothing I can do about the situation I am in. Right now is one of those nightmares, except for the horror of it being real.

Harry and Dave have got the canoes from behind the lookout hut into the water. Four red one-man canoes suddenly look like a lot of trouble for me.

'I don't want to—' I start, but Harry, who hasn't seemed to notice me this morning, drops his canoe and comes over.

'Don't worry, we're going to have a great time. We're going to test ourselves, and that is the biggest thrill of all.' He smooths my hair out of my eyes, and the gesture is so gentle and thoughtful I have to look at the ground to stop my eyes bombarding his with devotion.

I forget that I don't want the biggest thrill of all. I push the warnings I have learned since childhood out of my mind, and without further hesitation I step into the canoe Dave is holding for me. Immediately the current takes a hold and pulls me out into the sea behind Freda, who is paddling madly to stay in one place.

'This is so elemental,' she screams. 'Have you got any lip balm?'

'This is so bloody mental,' I shout back, doom heavy in my mind now I am out of the intoxicating aura of Harry's immediate presence.

Suddenly he sweeps by, Dave just behind him, and we are whisking along like Pooh-sticks on a swollen stream, except we are heading for the open sea. Harry paddles a circle, or attempts to and is brought up next to me. He looks serious for once.

'I've just realized we should have worn life jackets,' he says, then his eyes crease into a smile. 'But there is no way we can go back for them. Just you try paddling against this current.'

The panic that flows over me with his words has me gasping as if I have been dunked in icy water, and I try to turn my canoe, or even just bank it against the shore, desperate to stop, to escape this folly. But the current, as I know too well, has a pull like a juggernaut. It is useless to fight it, and exhausting to try.

The sun has vanished behind a cloud, and the sea has changed from blue to pewter. Dave's red T-shirt is vivid up ahead, drawing away from Freda in her pink summer top, a garment so fragile it looks completely out of place now the sea is rough.

We pass the lookout hut, and I stop pretending to myself that we will be fine and I shut my eyes and pray. I am really scared. I have never canoed round the end of the island before, because it is too dangerous. It is also very remote. Even Josh with his binoculars wouldn't see us up here if we needed rescuing, and anyway, who's to say that he's looking out for us at all today?

We are parallel with the dunes now. Soon we will be at the end of Salt Head and I have no idea how we are going to stop there. Seal Point is exposed for a short time, and we may not coincide with it. I have never tried to land on it, and have no idea how to, or how deep the water is when it comes in. I just know that it is treacherous. Freda and Dave are shouting and pointing in excitement, turning and wobbling in their canoes.

'A seal, a seal!'

'Look, it swam right past us. It's huge!'

Harry paddles enthusiastically to catch up.

'Come on, Lola, let's get a look at it.'

Their laughter on the wind reminds me of playtime at primary school and I think of Sadie. She will be coming out of infants now, happy but tired. She will go home with her mum and play in the garden or help hang out the laundry.

She will do what she does every day, and I will try to paddle for my life, with three people who have no idea of the danger they are in.

Here on Salt Head, the weather can alter in a flash. Now the sky has changed from summer afternoon azure to menacing, rumbling grey and brown.

The waves, which have been edged with a frill of white water, are suddenly peaks with stomach-swooping troughs, and the canoes scale them like model boats in a small child's bath. We are out by the very end of the island by this time, and although the light is gloomy and swampy, I can just make out the red line of rope fencing running around the peri-meter of the tern breeding area. My dad is the only person authorized to come up here, where the beach is littered with flints, and the rough sand and shallow bays look more like Scotland than Norfolk. He usually comes by motorboat, and as we spin past his mooring and the little jetty he has erected, with the red pole on which there is a lifebelt and a flare, I realize that I must act now, or we will be unable to save ourselves. I look around for the others, and it takes a moment to comprehend what I see. The sun has burst out from a tiny space in the banking dark cloud, and it glitters on the two canoes ahead of me. One, with Freda's pink top, darker now with sea spray, rides another huge wave, but the other has capsized, and there, next to it but not holding on, is the red blur of Dave.

'Harry! Harry!' I yell, turning wildly to find him. He is much nearer me than I thought, near enough for me to see the horror on his face.

'I'll try and get to him. You go for help, Lola,' he shouts.

'There isn't anywhere,' I scream back. 'We are miles away from everything. This end of Salt Head stretches back for miles. I'll send up a flare and maybe someone will see it.'

He doesn't reply. He is already ahead of me,

hunched over his paddle, the front of his canoe like a compass needle, aimed at Dave. Or rather Dave's canoe.

There is no sign of the red T-shirt in the heaving waters. I turn to the shore and try to paddle in. It is hopeless, impossible against the quickening tide. I am too far out.

'Oh my God,' I whimper, not even trying to paddle any more.

There is a thin shout from Freda. She is gesturing further out than I can bear to look. Dave has been swept on. He is treading water, and waving every few strokes. His head bobs, tiny and vulnerable on the swelling sea. Ignoring the empty canoe, Harry turns and paddles towards Dave but makes slow headway.

'This undertow is so powerful. Dave's got ahead and he's moving fast. I don't know if I can get to him,' he shouts.

'Just try,' I scream back. 'We've got to try.'

The wind is roaring in my ears, I can't hear anything but I can see Freda is mouthing something. She has turned her canoe, and is trying to paddle back towards me. She is not moving forward in the water. With utter disbelief, I watch her chuck her oar into the sea and jump in.

'What are you doing? You'll drown. You're mad!'

It looks as though she has drowned already, because as I speak a wave slaps over her and she disappears. A moment later she comes up in a completely different place, much nearer, gasping, chalk-white with hair sprawled down her face. And again she is submerged. Tears blur my vision, but I wipe them away furiously. I am witnessing someone drowning. This is what happened to my uncle. This is what my dad sees in his mind when he thinks of James. I look round wildly for Freda. She has not come up where I expected her. I can't see Dave either.

Freda appears further from me again, heading along the shore but about fifty metres out. Her canoe has floated away round the corner. Struggling, I paddle towards her. Her face is in the water, I do not take my eyes from her pink top floating. The rushing roar of the sea fills my ears, and my own voice, whispering over and over, 'She's going to be all right, she's going to be all right.'

I do not hear the boat engine, or see its looming bulk until I am no more than two waves from it.

Round from the seaward side of the point, dragging Freda's canoe, a fishing smack appears. It is Josh and his dad, Ian, and Billy Lawson coming in from a fishing trip. I am terrified that they are too late. A flare cracks into the sky, I can hear the fizz of the offshore radio and Ian giving urgent instructions.

'Get the lifeboat dinghy – they won't last more than twenty minutes and I don't know how many there are. I'll send up another flare for you to find us.'

Josh chucks a rope to me. It snakes into the water and lies rippling on the surface for a moment before I grab it and haul myself to the side of the boat. There I cling to the rope with one hand, gesturing with the other.

'It's not me, it's the others, quickly, please quickly.'

Billy reaches over and lifts me up by my armpits as if I am a small kitten.

He looks hard at me.

'Are any of you wearing life jackets?'

'No, and there are three others in the sea, not just me,' I gasp, then collapse, exhausted and over-whelmed, on a seat behind Josh.

Billy mutters something under his breath and moves away to scan the sea for the others. I am so wrung out that even when Josh strips off his weather-proof clothes, and, holding a rope, jumps off the other end of the boat in his shorts and life jacket, I cannot register any emotion at all. Dragging myself to my feet, I see him swimming with the rope towards the pink top, the only part of Freda with any colour in it.

'She's dead, she's dead,' I sob to Billy. 'And where are the others? They were there.'

'We will look for them when we've got this one in. The lifeboat is coming from Salt. It won't be long.'

'Dave's been in the water for ages already,' I whisper to myself more than anyone else.

'Christ, this is ever a job for the lifeboat men,' mutters Ian as he begins to haul Josh and the inert form of Freda back towards the boat. 'We've got to stop them both smacking themselves against the boat,' he says grimly to Billy. The pitching waves slap against the gunwales, and Ian leans right over into the sea, trying to keep the rope taut so Josh and Freda don't hit the side.

Billy leans with him and, after an eternity, Freda is hauled into the boat and Josh is pulled up behind

her. Freda is placed gently on the floor on the wet fishing nets. Billy covers her with his oilskin, Josh crouches over her, shivering, and administers the kiss of life. Nothing happens. A corner of my mind registers that the boat has turned and we are picking up speed, but I cannot risk looking away from Freda. Her skin is blue, and when Josh blows into her mouth, her cheeks swell then deflate again with a little pop. Her eyes are closed. Josh does not stop for a moment, does not hesitate, but pumps and blows, pumps and blows. All I can think is that Dave is still in the water, and Harry is there too. Freda must be gone already. Suddenly she struggles, turns her head and retches, vomiting bile and salt water. She sits up, gagging for breath, and sobs, 'I'm sorry, it was stupid to jump, but I couldn't stay in the canoe. I was being swept away, I just wanted to get out of the sea.'

I hadn't realized I was crying until I try to answer her.

'I thought you were trying to drown on purpose.'

Freda shakes her head, and starts to shake uncontrollably.

'Where's Dave? What are they doing?' she demands, her voice rising hysterically.

Josh wraps a towel around her shoulders.

'Here, Lola, take her down below deck. Give her some tea from Dad's flask. You'll find a jumper too.'

He opens the hatch into the small cabin, and Freda and I stumble down the steps into the warm, diesel-smelling hold.

'What about the boys?' Freda is trembling, jud-

dering like a washing machine. I put both arms round her.

'They'll be fine,' I soothe. 'They'll be fine.' I do not believe this, but I have to calm her down.

'Who will get them?'

'We will, I suppose.'

I can't tell her that we have rounded Seal Point and are tearing down the long beach where we swam only last night, away from the boys, back towards Salt. I cannot believe it myself, and all my thoughts are whirling through my head, shaping to one dreadful repeated image of a tiny canoe riding huge waves with no one in it.

Freda is silent, and has stopped shaking by the time we reach Salt. We wait on deck while Josh and Billy drop the anchors. The shingle beach is thronged with people, their stricken faces a freakish contrast to the summer dresses and bright T-shirts they are wearing. Little Sadie is holding her mum's hand, pulling her towards the front of the group, waving at me. In response, I try to uncurl my fingers from the blanket I have shrugged around me, but I cannot wave, and she cannot see.

Josh nudges me.

'Sadie's seen you,' he says. 'You'll be playing princesses with her again in a minute. Everything will be back to normal then.'

Coming in, with all these people watching, silent and shocked, is the most shaming moment in my life. I have been so stupid, and we have paid such a high price. My dad wades in the shallows for us, and I can hardly look at him I feel so ashamed and so frightened for the others. I am terrified that he will confirm that they are dead. His pale eyes tell me nothing. He has no reproach in his face, just loving concern.

'Here we are, girls. Just a few yards to dry land,' he says quietly. He lifts Freda across first and then turns to me. 'I'm glad you're back,' he says simply.

Freda stares at us in amazement. I think she expected more of a dramatic reunion considering I have been snatched from the jaws of death. I reach to put my arms round Dad's neck and I hug him as tight as I can.

'Let's get you on to the beach,' says Dad, and we wade out of the sea behind Josh, who has jumped into the water to help secure the boat in the rough sea. Caroline pushes through the crowd.

'I think this is the moment to lay old ghosts to rest,' she says, and instead of hugging me, or Josh, or even her husband, who is standing, looking sheepish in the shallows in his waders, she hugs Dad. Even more weirdly, he hugs her back and real tears stand in his eyes.

'Thank you all for this.' He turns to Josh and his dad, clapping his hands on each of their shoulders then pulling them awkwardly together so he is embracing both of them. 'Thank you. I stand now and forever in your debt,' he says, and both he and Josh's dad get out huge handkerchiefs and blow their noses.

Grandma suddenly appears, fear still draining her face of colour. She cups her hands around my head and looks searchingly at me.

'Oh, Lola, my dear Lola,' she says. 'I thought we'd lost you. I must thank the Christies.'

I struggle to free myself; all this gratitude, and Harry and Dave are still missing. I have to tell her.

'The boys are still out there, and Dave was in the water—'

'Where are the boys?'

Mr Lascalles is suddenly at the front of the crowd with Pansy and Jessie; they are each holding on to one of his arms, as if he cannot stand without them. His voice is sharp with anxiety. Billy, still on the boat, hears him and shouts an answer.

'They're coming in now in the lifeboat. They're both all right, I've spoken to the skipper on the radio.'

With a blanket wrapped around me, and Dad's arm steering me through the crowd, I am feeling stronger every second. And light-headed. The orange lifeboat dinghy bouncing on the waves, with the afternoon sun behind it, is a beacon of hope, delivering weedy Dave and Harry back to the land. Mr Lascalles and Pansy and Jessie wade into the water to meet them, with Carl and Pete just behind, offering to piggyback them in. Harry laughs, and jumps off the lifeboat into the shallows, where he greets Josh and they shake hands then hug. Dave is still very weak and coughing a lot, so he is lifted above the water to the shingle beach. No one speaks. It has been too immense an experience for conversation.

Gradually the crowd drifts away, and the grey turbulence of the early afternoon dissolves into a still, hazy summer day. The sea is smooth as glass now, only the low sunlight sending sparks like a shiver

across the blue stillness. It is beautiful and beguiling, beckoning. I know it has already won me back, but I'm not so sure about the others. Only time will tell.

A sea tragedy was narrowly averted this week when freak weather caught a group of young people by surprise. Former local girl Lola Jordan, 14, was canoeing round the Point with companions from the James Ellis Grammar School, Harry Sykes, 17, Freda Low, 14, and Dave Fisher, 15, when the storm blew up. 'We were paddling on an outgoing tide and we couldn't get in,' explains Lola, who is the daughter of Conservation Warden Richard Jordan. Lola and her schoolmates struggled against ten-foot waves and were heading out over exposed Seal Point, with two of them in the water before rescuers were alerted. They are lucky to be alive.

In an eerie echo of the past, we can reveal that the drama unfolded on exactly the same stretch of water where Richard Jordan's elder brother James was drowned, aged 15, in 1969. On that terrible day James was crewing for Ian Christie, when a similar freak storm blew up and his boat capsized. Ian, knocked unconscious, was washed up on Seal Point, where Jack Jordan rescued him, sailing with expert precision over Seal Point as it was submerged beneath the tide. His own son James's body was recovered several days later beyond Salt. History has gone full circle today; it was Ian Christie, now 50, who with his son Josh, 17, performed the courageous rescue of the girls today. The boys, Harry and Dave, were brought to safety by the lifeboat crew just moments after the girls had been taken on board Christie's boat *The Little Princess*.

The two families, who have lived in the area for decades, with Jack Jordan presiding over the sailing club until his death this year, are unanimous in agreeing that the rift created by the terrible sorrow of that long-ago tragedy has been well and truly healed today.

The parents of the James Ellis Grammar School children have shown their gratitude by setting up a trust to fund a full-time coastguard on the Point. There are plans to start a summer school too, to bring urban children to the sea so they can learn to respect this unfamiliar environment. Josh Christie is hotly tipped as the best man to run the project.

EPILOGUE

We don't exactly abandon the field trip after this, instead we all go and stay at my house for the next two nights and Caroline Christie and Grandma cook us endless meals. No one talks much, but the atmosphere is full of relief. On Monday morning I get up early because we are leaving for London today. Cactus and I walk along the coast path towards Hinkley Marshes, and the noise of the gulls and the sea whispering is familiar and safe in the morning sun. I sit on the sand by the water's edge while Cactus careers through the samphire behind me and I am almost floating with thankfulness that everything has turned out all right.

I can't believe now that I thought I was going to die, or that the others were in such danger. It wasn't even surprising to me when Josh and Ian arrived in their boat, but actually it was a miracle, and we would have drowned if they had not come at that moment. Dad has been amazing. I thought he would be so angry because we did everything we shouldn't, but in fact I think he is so overcome with gladness, and now he has made up with Caroline and Ian. They came for supper last night, and Grandma was here too. A friendship that seemed impossible just a few days ago is suddenly normal and I saw Grandma wiping her eyes with her handkerchief, and Caroline hugging her and it was like a weight off my shoulders that I didn't know I was carrying.

At supper I sat between Josh and Harry and they both teased me, but Josh was like a brother, the brother I always wanted. Harry, though, is something else. I'm not sure what yet, but it's exciting and I don't think it's just a holiday thing. Maybe we are going out together. I'm not sure, but there's time to find out and the future looks exciting. I'm glad to be going back to London with him and all the others. Staitheley is here for me, with all my past, and I have learned that I can have both worlds now.

Cactus bounds up and jumps on to my lap. He wriggles and wags his tail, delighted and wanting to let me know he has rolled in something. I don't need him this close to realize it is something rank. He has covered me in it too. I leap up and take off my jeans and without pausing I run, carrying Cactus, into the sea and dive underwater. It is the best, most exhilarating feeling I know.

A selected list of titles
available from Macmillan Children's Books

The prices shown below are correct at the time of going to press.
However, Macmillan Publishers reserves the right to show new retail
prices on covers which may differ from those previously advertised.

Jaclyn Moriarty

| Feeling Sorry for Celia | 0 330 39725 7 | £5.99 |
| Finding Cassie Crazy | 0 330 41803 3 | £5.99 |

Caroline B. Cooney

Burning Up	0 330 39104 6	£4.99
Mercy	0 330 40015 0	£4.99
On the Seas to Troy	0 330 41519 0	£4.99

Cynthia D. Grant

| Cannibals | 0 330 42044 5 | £4.99 |

Rose Wilkins

| So Super Starry | 0 330 42087 9 | £4.99 |
| So Super Stylish | 0 330 43452 7 | £9.99 |

All Pan Macmillan titles can be ordered from our website,
www.panmacmillan.com, or from your local bookshop
and are also available by post from:

Bookpost, PO Box 29, Douglas, Isle of Man IM99 1BQ

Credit cards accepted. For details:
Telephone: 01624 677237
Fax: 01624 670923
Email: bookshop@enterprise.net
www.bookpost.co.uk

Free postage and packing in the United Kingdom